Two Women

by

Nicholas Leigh

First published 2013

Published by Liborwich Publishing

Contact us at:
liborwichpublishing@gmail.com

Dedicated to

Dan and Martine,
Gabriella and Sam

<u>1</u>

She loved both her parents dearly, but it was losing her mother that she'd feared the most, from the very first inkling it was possible. Her father: a success, a man of integrity and substance; from the age of three she knew this to be true. But remote: a presence only in passing, silent to the point of severe. For hugs, affection and warmth she'd always turned to her mother, who was superb at providing these finite resources to anyone in need, and not just her only child. The woman most liked in any sphere she inhabited, capable of putting everyone at ease and finding common ground with any stranger. A life force whose energy filled the room, her daughter fearless at being so well protected, so well loved, but for that one, ghastly possibility, that one day her mother may be gone. Though she knew she'd suffer if her father died, it was the loss of her mother that would mean the loss of her own life too. She confessed this to no-one; any way, they'd have said it was impossible that such a dynamic spirit could be quietened within at least the next century.

And now Cassie stood, eleven years old on a day drained of colour, at the edge of the grave into which her mother's coffin had just been lowered. All was quiet, even the air muted, stilled by tragedy. A great turnout; one would expect nothing less for someone so young, so popular as Lucy. But being the focus of so much heartbreak, so many glances, was a trial in itself for the little girl, an intense discomfort in a field of the cold and dead. Cassie absorbed the expressions of sadness, an archivist of her lost mother's renown, but each made her feel worse until she was certain that the next furrowed brow or pursed lip or slight shake of the head or murmur of apology would make her brain explode. She looked at her father, who'd been consumed by a quiet, closed grief that had settled into his bones in the months before cancer had murdered his wife, and which had hardened into a cocoon of anguish in the days since. He'd said nothing to Cassie after Lucy had closed her eyes for the last time, and moved on to a place beyond contact, beyond reach. He'd barely even looked at her since, his only child, and when he did, his eyes were devoid of fatherliness or humanity. Now he stared at the portion of the earth into which Lucy had been placed, and over which heavy soil would soon be thrown, hiding her forever.

Bereft of her broken father, Cassie glanced across the nearby gravestones. Each spoke of its own despair, but she had no energy for their baggage: they were not her mother, her great friend, her beloved entertainer, her wise counsel. They were strangers to the little girl: she couldn't touch or feel their calamity, only see its lonely monument, mildew on the stone, the silent wearing away of supposedly eternal words. Likewise, they were not concerned by her loss, though she could think of nothing else. The prospect of having no one to ask her silly questions; no one to assist her when dressing and she didn't know what to wear; no one to make dinner whenever she felt hungry, whatever time of the day or night; no one to know what she wanted to ask but couldn't, or reply with sage advice; no one to look at her the way other mothers would look at their children ... She despised this endless array of "no ones", and no amount of sympathy from strangers would settle a sense that anything other than the world had ended. The dead air of the cemetery combined with her father's motionless expression to inform her that without doubt she was truly alone.

After the burial, she continued to be spoken of as a tragic child by people close enough to hear. And still more traces of the woman her mother had been, in the grief of strangers, the echoes of shocked faces. Cassie walked through a crowd impossible to get lost in, though she tried hard to vanish between the long legs and fine threads. Her father sat on a chair in the corner of the room, unable to speak or cry. Those caught between the two had difficulty determining who seemed worse off: the widower brought to an existential halt or the child threatened by a future so different from her past. Even those sympathetic to Hugo would acknowledge that Lucy was the warm one, and that the young girl would feel as if all the lights in the house had gone out. But sympathy lasts only as long as the sympathetic are in the room. Gradually the mourners left and, as Cassie feared, finally it was just she and her father and the house and no one else. She looked at him for any kind of word or gesture. Neither came, only a frozen stare, before he disappeared into his chair in the lounge, which overlooked the vast field onto which the back of the house gazed, a mythic vista. In winter, the rain and hard breeze would curl across the peak of the horizon, whilst in summer the outcrops of trees provided subtle shade from the sun. A field in which children could run and run and still be safe, and parents host lavish parties which disturbed no one else. A field for a family in love, and ice cold in its absence. Eventually driven away by his wintriness, Cassie left for bed, where she lay, her door closed, crying brittle, extravagant tears.

She woke in the middle of the night with a stab of shock that she hadn't dreamt of her mother, immediately beset by the shame of disloyalty. The only way she'd ever be able to see or speak to Lucy again would be in dreams. Yet already she'd proven unreceptive to attempts Lucy might have made to visit her in this most select arena. Was she out in the cold of the void alone, knocking on the doors of her daughter's consciousness, only to find this sole portal shut, and locked? Could she see the life taken from her, the daughter she'd cherished, the husband she alone understood, still in the land of the living from which she'd been dragged forever? Worst of all, had she craved a smile from Cassie, a simple token of affection, nothing more, but was denied even this sliver of love because her daughter hadn't let her in? Overcome by self-hatred, the eleven year old spent the remaining hours til sunrise berating herself, sobbing in pain at the thought of Lucy returning to the void with a sense of having been forgotten by those she had loved the most.

Exhausted, Cassie made breakfast for herself, Hugo too, but her father didn't touch his; she only ate a couple of mouthfuls of hers. In the six months from terminal diagnosis to death, fearful for Hugo's physical health as well as his mental state, Lucy had tried to teach Cassie as much as she could about the basics of survival, including how to feed herself, knowing that she'd be able to feed her father too if, as she suspected, he became completely incapable. Cassie – like both of her parents fiercely intelligent – learnt fast, and nowadays could cook pretty well for an eleven-year-old. But regardless of how impressive her culinary skills may be, Hugo seemed content to fade away, to vanish along with Lucy, as fast as he could. Cassie cleaned up the plates, no appetite at all.

The house was woundingly silent. Hugo didn't speak, to Cassie or anyone else; never much of a talker before the cancer, there was little point in trying to engage him in conversation now, for he'd just not respond. If the phone rang, he'd ignore it; if she left it for him to pick up, eventually she'd be driven to distraction by the relentless ringtone and take the call. Soon most people realised he was unavailable at that or any other number, and stopped trying. And so the silent house became even more somnolent. Her mother, the ringleader of mischief: her vanishing had taken too the spirit of fun.

The empty day lay ahead of them, with nothing to fill it. Open-ended leave from his firm distanced Hugo from the only occupation that could calm his pre-occupation. His daughter had doubts that sitting at home like a piece of old furniture was best for his health. She'd similarly been let off school for as long as she required, felt fine for much of the time, but would suddenly start to cry and not be able to stop. This was to be expected, but she'd also developed a habit witnesses invariably found disturbing. Instead of sobbing, she'd start to spill a stream of consciousness, leaping unstoppably from subject to subject in a coherent fashion at a pace of hundreds of words per minute, for 15 or 20 minutes, after which she'd run dry, distressed and exhausted, to her relief as much as others'. This babbling began with a comment of no importance, such as how she liked raspberries more than cherries, and then would rocket off at speed through a dozen subjects before stating with certainty that dogs had souls but cats did not. The strange habit began a few weeks after Lucy was diagnosed as a terminal case, and alarmed her mother more than anything else. With sage accuracy, she mused that Cassie was trying to say as much as she could to her in the time before she died. But the habit continued after Lucy had gone, leaving unsuspecting passers-by with the impression the child was possessed.

There'd been plenty of grief without the addition of such strain. Lucy hadn't had to be told that something was terribly wrong with her body: her cells knew she'd been stricken by an inescapable disease. When the doctor said she had a cancer that would kill her within six-to-twelve months, she smiled a casual tell me something I don't know!! A bravado at odds with the calamity, during her illness, she was honest with her husband and daughter about her zero prospects of survival, and encouraged them to "stock up" on her while she was still around, to make as many memories as they could in the time available – she'd provide them with all the energy at her disposal. In making these memories, Cassie and Lucy had some great times, but couldn't escape the distant drumming, the reason for the exercise.

Meanwhile, Hugo was unable to climb out from beneath the burdens of work to make a store of his own; others grumbled that he was ignoring the inevitable. Cassie was the opposite: she wanted her mother for as long as possible, to make as many recollections over as wide a range of activities as they could in the little time they had left.

After the diagnosis, and before she became too ill to drive, Lucy took Cassie to places she had loved as a child. On a mini-road trip, mother and daughter yakked away non-stop, with Cassie recording the whole day on her mobile phone, hours and hours of footage of them both. They talked on the drive there; they talked while walking around wherever they'd landed – be it a small town, seaside, or city; they talked while having ice cream in cafés where Lucy's stylish headscarf worn to hide the cruelty of chemotherapy drew looks of kind concern; they talked on the drive home and for another three hours when they got back, until Cassie fell asleep mid-sentence, pooped but unwilling to stop. For this most important business, Lucy found reserves of energy she wouldn't otherwise have had, the cancer draining her without rest – but for this cause, her willpower exceeded human awesomeness, and though the sheer greyness of her skin could register in the footage, so too did the fight behind her eyes. Yet death gave plenty of reminders that it would have its way, and so the mother would have to take pause, get her breath, lay down, recover as well she could, underneath the terrified gaze of her child. These moments of quiet desperation punctuated their outings, never less than a fact of hours away, but then would come the rising, however transitory, and they'd do it all over again the next day, until the time came when Lucy was too ill to leave the house.

She regaled her daughter with tales of her childhood, recollections of family members, all the history she could think of, even her relationship with Hugo – anything that may be of future aid to her soon-to-be-motherless daughter. Life lessons, top ten lists, advice, quotes that made her chuckle and think. Soon Cassie accumulated a grand stock of her mother's voice, glances, looks and smiles. She transferred gigantic amounts of mobile phone footage onto her computer, where she carefully titled each of the files with a few words by way of content and the date it was shot. She saved the electronic library to a back-up hard drive, and for insurance saved it all again to another, which she placed in the furthest coolest confines of her wardrobe with the same care as one may handle volatile nuclear material. Sometimes, a day or two later, Lucy would remember a few more nuggets of life she'd forgotten to impart and wanted to share, so they'd pick up the subject where they'd left off, and the daughter would film it and then file that extra, precious footage along with the original batch and all the various back-ups.

The eleven-year-old collected quite a store of stock, yet both mother and daughter knew they'd never manage to cover even a fraction of all Cassie would need to know as she travelled along the twisting, menacing, hazardous roads of life.

As a lark, in the benighted period between when her parents caved in and bought her a mobile phone and when Lucy was diagnosed with cancer, mother and daughter would often send each other jokes, silly texts, hidden teasings of Hugo, who could be sitting in the room and have no idea why they would explode in hysterics. The siren of the arrival of a text message would sound from Cassie's phone, a triple-tone; she'd look at the message, from "Mum"; open it, read it and howl in delight; Lucy would laugh at Cassie's reaction, and a suspicious glare would depart from Hugo; he knew he was being made the butt of a joke. After the onset of Lucy's disease, there were still a great many texts, including those making fun of him. Finally, inevitably, Lucy became too weak to use her phone, and the japery stopped, a week before she died. By then Cassie had saved many text messages. Re-reading them now made her fall about laughing and crying at the same time.

A hard, sharp contrast with the context of her life in this house of new obscurity. Nothing lived within these walls. Cassie longed for a cat, her life marginally more bearable if she had another little creature to share her space with, a cute, sleek animal with whom she could prowl around the house, she sneaking up on the cat, the cat sneaking up on her; she'd look after it, expect no custodial commitment from her father, would feed, domesticate and clean up after it, and put it out at night and let it in the following morning; the cat would slink into her room and sleep on her bed and purr softly and wake her up and gently demand feeding by licking her face and they would be best buds and she would always respect her cat's privacy and never let a dog into the house ... but she had asked Hugo and he'd not even said no, he'd stared at her with such an abyss of a blank expression that she felt like an evil little demon child to have made such a suggestion so soon after the death of her mother. And that was that, case closed, no cat, not now, not ever, and don't you dare ask me again.

In this fashion, the unused days and weeks after Lucy's death cranked by endlessly, each passing with the gloom of eternal slowness, with no more of her smiles or raucous chuckle. Visitors stopped visiting less and less, with respects already paid and the atmosphere in the house of mourning as great a deterrent to the casual passer-by as was known to humankind; the silent widower and haunted, perhaps possessed child didn't exactly scream out party time. Often, the silence was broken only if Hugo simply had to take a call, a matter of life and death. He'd respond in monosyllables, grunts, sighs, stares, long silences ... He'd be as dead-tongued as Cassie was verbose, and the caller would likely not ring back again.

In the night, the hard edge of bereavement came, when regardless of however many memories of Lucy she'd collected in her store they were still not enough to quench the eleven-year-old's need for her mother to be close, to be there, in the room, a present presence, not a presence in absentia, a mere compilation of fragments. If the days were slow, the nights stood still. Cassie would look at the clock on her mobile phone, the last ten minutes having taken an hour to pass. She'd stand from her bed and walk around the room, at which point time would halt completely beneath her feet. The longer she walked, the more obstinate her clock's resistance to advance by even a second. A mockery made of this shattered child by the mechanics of perception, only when she climbed back in to bed would the hands of the clock deign to proceed again with a forward motion, however slowly. The morning that broke found the child dozing, having dropped off for a few hours, sleep at last but far less than she needed before the whole depressing cycle began anew.

2

An essay in pre-teen boredom, Cassie sat in the back seat of her aunt's car, staring out of the window at the visible monotony of a long trip. Arlene, Hugo's younger sister, had taken it upon herself to liberate (temporarily at least) her only niece from the debilitating claustrophobia of the airless mausoleum the house of mourning had become; even an insensitive huckster could see it was no place for an eleven-year-old to thrive. Arlene was appalled by the evaporating, nocturnal pallor that had befallen Hugo and Cassie in such a short space of time. Her brother was a poor communicator, his career success based on what he said, not how he said it. In all other matters, he'd relied upon Lucy to interpret for him, in social circumstances, in family dealings ... Now she was gone he was back to being the mute she knew from childhood: taciturn to the point of discourteous, you daren't attempt a joke, for the gag hadn't been written that could puncture his ponderous gravity, so why even try? Lucy had freed Hugo; but despite being grateful that someone had rescued her brother, Arlene could never work out why her sister-in-law had bothered, for there are some things that even love can't take the rap for. She'd forgotten how deeply he could withdraw into himself, how unnerving it was for civilians. Arlene acclimatised to this flagrant aridity whilst growing up, but Cassie had never seen him disappear so utterly. Now she was providing her niece with respite, delighted at being able to help the little girl she'd always loved but towards whom she'd felt superfluous in the presence of Lucy.

Would that it seemed like a liberation to Cassie. Her aunt was interesting and friendly and knew the journey well, but none of it registered, apart from the trees passing rapidly, as if they were being catapulted in the opposite direction. She seemed to have taken Hugo's gloom with her; it wouldn't be so easy to escape, and why should it? The gloom belonged to her too; if she could drive away from it, she'd never go back. Absently, she started to count the trees flying past. Once underway, she couldn't stop. Arlene eventually accepted that Cassie had zoned out, had left the realm of the car for her own lumber-numeric world. As the purpose of the trip was to help her niece relax, she let her be. By the time they reached their destination, Cassie had counted more than five hundred trees. She was strangely satisfied by the achievement.

In her industry, she hadn't noticed their arrival in a lovely little town, set by a picturesque river, with a stylish guest house: their home for the next couple of days. The lady at the reception was extraordinarily friendly, and there was a delightful scent about the place, a freshness Cassie appreciated. Arlene had booked them a room each — "because you're a woman now", she had said - with a connecting door in case she turned out in the middle of the night to be not quite such a woman after all. A key of her own, she arranged with her auntie to settle in and then they'd go exploring.

Entering her private realm, Cassie lay on the bed. Arlene had brought her to such a beautiful place that she started to feel guilty about ignoring her on the outbound journey. So many pretty little things in this room, ideal for a young woman, yes, a woman now, a grown up, a veteran of bereavement. Cassie stretched herself off the bed, wandered around, looking at everything at her disposal, and the river view from the window. The afternoon sunshine rendered her reflection burnished as she passed the long mirror. She unpacked, secretly pleased at how neat her clothes looked, as flat as when they went in. A precision she had inherited from her father, though she was in no mood to give him credit for anything. She started to place her clothes in the wardrobe, carefully allocating hangers and drawers. And then she began to babble.

`Nooooo!!!` she yelled in despair, before her words and new-found peace were subsumed by her own brand of madness. Not yet a witness to the lunacy, she didn't want Arlene to think she'd be spending the weekend with a dangerous freak bent crazy by grief, but that's how it would appear to any objective judge. The usual random rubbish began to spout forth, she was unable to control it, and now in a small, unfamiliar room with nowhere to run, talking to the wall, talking to the wardrobe, talking to the mirror, a new breed of wacko, she hoped to exhaust this attack away from her aunt's eyes and not be struck again while they were together. Her face became flush, with embarrassment, with fear. The babbling rocked her whole body; a hands-off beating from an invisible assailant, and once started, wouldn't stop until done. She began to cry, beset by the misfortunes of suffering pointless, relentless prolix and emotional exhaustion, brutalised by the withering cosmos. Eventually, after twenty minutes of nuttiness, the babbling came to a sudden, random end, releasing her from its torture. She fell onto the bed shattered, and slept like the baby she'd never again be, for she was a woman now.

`I'm sorry I woke you,` Arlene said, as they sat in the restaurant later.

`It's fine,` the eleven-year-old replied.

`I was starting to get worried. We said three o'clock.`

`I'm sorry.`

Her aunt smiled. `Listen, don't worry about it, it's fine. I'm glad you had some sleep. Do you feel better for the nap?`

`A little.`

Arlene looked around the restaurant. `You know, your dad and I used to come here. A close friend of our mother once owned it. Hugo was old enough to look after me, so mother would send us here just the two of us on our own.`

`Huh,` Cassie sneered. `That explains a lot.`

Arlene smiled. `Yeah, our mother wasn't like your mother; your dad takes a lot of understanding. Lucy was good at that.`

Cassie nodded. Her left eye flickered, a twitch.

`You're not sleeping well, are you.`

Niece looked at aunt. Her instinct was to lie; she was adept at providing adults with answers they wanted – but she realised what Arlene meant when she called her a woman. The mild lesson took her by surprise and, so taught, she shook her head.

A look of dazzling affection passed across Arlene's face, the first firebomb of love the child had received since her mother had died. She felt a leap of filial gratitude equal to the stimulus: someone likes me after all! But then accused herself of shocking disloyalty, the mere act of responding to her aunt's kindness tantamount to forgetting her mother. Arlene's expression remained aglow; she could feed off this kindness for days. Arlene was childless, a recent divorcee. She and Lucy had been friends, but maybe something had been said long ago, and the mix soured. Whatever the reason, Arlene hadn't been a big part of Cassie's life, and now it felt to Cassie as if she were trying to bridge that gap, under the guise of a mercy mission. Trying to do more, trying to make the gulf disappear, as if never there, but to do so would imply Lucy had never been there, that Cassie was born a motherless child, and now Arlene could assume the maternal mantle, and by doing so plug the unforgiving chasm in her own life. The eleven-year-old was no fool. Cassie fixed Arlene with a tough stare. Okay then, she thought, woman to woman: what do you want from me?

Arlene was still beaming at her, radiating the warmth of a beautiful day on a beach with the sea lapping gently and the ice cream flowing freely. Cassie realised she was unable to defend herself against such powerful good vibes. Ripe with determined anger, the eleven-year-old stated, `I like the steak,` choosing the most expensive item on the menu, hoping to break the spell. `I'll have mine medium rare.`

Arlene nodded, no shudder at the cost but delighted by her niece's hearty appetite. `Excellent!` she said, `My little carnivore! This weekend is for eating and sleeping and talking and fun! And for pretending that silent blocks of stone called Hugo don't exist.`

The eleven-year-old chuckled, in spite of herself; she told herself off for chuckling.

Her campaign against Arlene was weakened further by how much she enjoyed the dinner that followed. Wise and witty, indiscreet and naughty, aunt bombarded niece with care and warmth, and soon the guilty thoughts were passing, and Cassie was indeed relaxing away from the brooding menace of her father. In the aftermath of her suspicion, tales of romance and adventure spiced up with gossip and dramatic detail transported the child to other lands, places she wanted to go as a child, as a woman. Arlene told tales as if Cassie was already a part of them, two women together, competing with the men, beating the men, having them fall at their feet. In trying hard to detect the ulterior motive in her aunt's many expressions, Cassie had to concede that she wore a damn effective mask.

Her delightfully comfortable bed provided Cassie with a perfect platform on which to break her heart. She was ready to sleep for many hours - Arlene was right about that – but grief continued to shake her without warning, and desperately so. Alone in her room after they'd retired for the night, she sobbed relentlessly. Cassie needed no reason for a spontaneous outbreak of tears, but she was often too tired to burn energy she didn't have on emotions that couldn't be quelled. She rocked with the force of her crying, the duvet crumpling untidily around her, a boa constrictor limiting her movements until she was trapped, her arms and legs bound by heartache, a sarcophagus of a girl, inside of which there used to be a happy, boundless Cassie. Either the emotion or the energy gave way, the duvet loosening around her, and she fell into a long, deep sleep. Just as she was going under, she tried to dream, to leave the door wide open for Lucy to come and visit, to hug and kiss and tell her about Heaven, and they could laugh and joke about Hugo and Cassie could reassure her mother that she knew Arlene's plan, and there was no way she'd ever replace her in the bereaved girl's life. But when Cassie slept, her slumber was so heavy that she sank too deep for dreams, and any visitation by Lucy again went unnoticed.

From beneath many layers, a distant yet familiar sound ... So rare in recent weeks. Then nothing.

And there it was again! Cassie couldn't tell if a few minutes or a few years had passed between the first and second buzz. Half asleep, she was awake enough to reach out for her phone, perched by the side of her bed. Eyes barely open, she lifted her head an inch from the pillow.

She blinked and looked, saw a text message which read: "If you need me, just say. I am here for you, always xx"

She squinted hard, the blurry words taking a long moment to make their way through her eyes and into her brain. Eventually the content of the message registered. `Wha ...?` she breathed, in the far distance of the room.

Emblazoned in the banner at the top of the text, she looked at the sender's name:

"Mum".

Cassie sat bolt upright, the text pulsating with fervid dismay. Staring at the text, her eyes wide open, there in the dark, she started to tremble, far from home, the unchanging words, the unchanging name, a cruel, bizarre trick, a mistake??? She hit the lamp, the room became light but dark still pushed from behind the curtains, the near garish, circus-like, the night going nowhere yet.

She glanced at the clock on the phone. 2.32am. She'd slept for more than four hours; the additional ten she'd hoped for evaporated feebly into the lamplight. The strain upon her narrow shoulders fell from a height past the moon, landing with chronic impact, everything contained within: the struggle of trying to look after her father though he clearly didn't want her to; the strain of trying to look after herself though she was only eleven; the strain of resisting her aunt's irresistible affections; she might as well lay back on the bed and never get up. And now this. She slammed her phone down on the bedside cabinet, switched off the lamp, turned her back on the text and tried to will herself to sleep.

But the words of the text – the name of its sender – glowed fluorescent between her eyelids and her eyes: there it was, whichever way she turned, however consumed by her duvet. A sweaty, feverish feeling, a shrill carnival blaring in her ears, impossible to sleep with such a racket. Carrying fatigue which at home kept her frazzled, but here, far away, was almost like someone else's problem, happening to a stranger, she could just close her eyes and it would be gone and ...

To her surprise, she woke again at 5am, yet still flattened by her sleep, beset by a surge of waking nerves. Immediately the text filled her mind. She wondered if she'd dreamt at last, and that rather than seeing her mother again she'd imagined the text. Cassie seized her phone in the dark and drew it into bed with her. Under the covers, she keyed her way to her messages, the screen illuminating the cave created by the duvet, her heartbeat cacophonous. And there it was, no dream, but real:

If you need me, just say: I am here for you, always xx.

And the sender's name:

Mum.

The bed was about to swallow her. Cassie was sure she'd sink into a bundle enclosed by the valance sheet, only for the maid to come in the next morning, turn out the mattress and find it empty, the little girl vanished. She began to cry, for not only did she not know how this message had found its way onto her mobile phone, but also from the pangs that she wished it were true, that her mother really was trying to contact her from beyond the grave. She was no baby, but no fool either: her Mum was dead, she was gone forever, so what if comatose Hugo hadn't been able to get his head around that: she had. Yet someone had sent this text. With a temper she'd have thought beyond her, she leapt out of bed and cursed a streak of obscenities that could scar the pristine paintwork, the lavender wallpaper, hissed in an undertone, a spell of voodoo vengeance, a curse upon nothing and all, to debilitate her frustration. Then, as always, the words ran out, the tears ran out, the babbling ran out, and she was alone in the silence, the dark and the night.

She fainted; at least, that's what she thought had happened, because at one point she was standing and the next thing she knew she was sprawled on the floor, her left side sore but her head fine – she'd fallen well. She knew she should get up, but had no energy, no drive to achieve that simple outcome. So she lay in the middle of the room, thinking about the text, thinking about nothing.

And then into her mind popped a conversation she'd had with Andrew Faro, the family's lawyer, soon after Lucy had died. Faro had called her a few days after her mother's funeral to say Lucy had wanted him to have a word with Cassie about arrangements. He explained to the eleven-year-old the process regarding her mother's will and the administration of her estate; Lucy intuited that Hugo wouldn't be able to guide his daughter through this minefield of adult business. Independently wealthy of her husband, most of her estate would pass to Hugo but Cassie had inherited 25%, to be held in trust until she was eighteen; the trustee being Andrew, not her father.

`Did she tell you ... how much that would work out to be?` Faro asked.

Cassie shook her head, the first she had ever heard of this.

`You've inherited more than two million,` the lawyer said.

She knew it was a lot of money, more than she'd ever need, but past that, it registered as no more than a reminder that her mother was gone forever. Cassie would have much rather had Lucy, and let her mother keep her more than two million.

Faro continued. `There are personal items that belonged to her that she wanted you to have. Then there's the usual sorting out, trivia really, but stuff she didn't want you to worry about ... I'll take care of everything.`

Cassie liked the way he spoke: a soft tone underlaid with gravitas, the only echo of security she could find in this horrid time. She began to well up, tears pooling in her eyes though nothing else about her moved.

`I'm not going to say it'll be alright,` Faro said. `It will never be the same again. You'll miss her like crazy. But after each day comes another, and another. And then one day you'll be a mother yourself. And in the things you do for your own children, that's when you'll find Lucy again.`

3

When Arlene brought her niece home at the end of their weekend, Hugo looked at Cassie with more than a blank for the first time since her mother's death. This would have been good news had his expression been any less disconcerting. An aggressive stare, dead eyes, the rest of his face unmoving. And so: the first sign of emotion she'd received from her grief-stricken father turned out to be antagonistic. She hadn't even taken off her coat and already she wished she were far away. Intimidated and angry in equal measure, she rushed past Hugo to her bedroom, where she slammed the door so loudly the impact could be heard in every register of the house.

On the drive back, Arlene had tried to be too nice. Cassie hadn't told her about the text message (which followed her around for the entire weekend like a malevolent imp – yet she couldn't help looking at it every couple of hours). She hadn't told Arlene much at all, including how she'd really enjoyed herself, thankful for the relief of being away from her father, from her cavernous, cold home, and how she'd adored being treated like a grown up – like a woman. There'd been treats a-plenty, long walks through beautiful countryside, a plastic-punishing shopping trip, her first glass of wine. Cassie loved Arlene's comical and embarrassing stories of Hugo;

her aunt segued through narratives that bereft of strain and speed could be deemed the distant cousin of her niece's babbling, a chip off the near block if not the old block. Yet it was her obvious desire to entertain Cassie and improve her mood that prevented the eleven-year-old from saying that it had worked to such a powerful degree. She realised how messed up that was.

So, with good vibes dissipated by the gloom of the house of mourning, Cassie was back in solitary confinement, a Papillion on her own Devil's Island. The petrified manse an environment to endure, her father wandered around like a ghost haunting his own life, slowly fading into the long shadows that reached around corners. She could walk the perimeter but still there would be no contact, no word from others. There were views from windows but their house was set way back from the road, and, detached, had no immediate neighbours with whom to pass the time of day. Lucy made sure she saw her school friends, but Hugo was as vanished as she, so Cassie couldn't even get out to play, while the parents of her friends were wary of dealing with the stonewall of tragedy Hugo represented, as the child had been taken out of her classes and had yet to return. Though Cassie would still exchange texts with her pals, actual contact was limited to nil.

Repressed and depressed in equal measure, her mind was seized by thoughts of the text, what to do about it, where it may have come from, who on earth had sent it ... She had been an efficient five-year-old, demanding no more toys to play with than she required and able to make a bar of chocolate last all day; she'd been an efficient nine-year-old: at birthday parties apportioning soft drinks fairly and enjoying making new clothes by cannibalising unwanted dresses, jeans, whatever. At the grand old age of eleven, it was no surprise she remained as efficient.

`Cassie!` said Faro, answering the phone to the little person who was rapidly becoming his favourite client. `My dear, how are you getting on?`

`I'm okay,` she replied. `Andrew: can I check something?`

`Of course!`

A few days had passed since the weekend away, and the eleven-year-old's thinking had wandered into obscure territory which may nevertheless have been crucial to recent events. `When you were sorting out the stuff to do with my Mum, including all the little bits, did you cancel her ... her mobile phone contract?`

Cassie's efficiency took even the lawyer by surprise. `Well, yes, I did.`

`When would that have been?`

`Oh ... A couple of weeks after your mother ... after she passed away, so I suppose ... getting on for two months ago.`

`Umm ... Okay: thanks.`

`Was that all?`

`Yup.`

Faro was glad to be of help, but troubled by the distant, faded sound of her voice. `Cassie: how are you doing?`

`Yeah, I'm okay.`

`Are you sure? Are you getting enough sleep ...?`

The care in his voice sounded like a spiritual balm, a cleanser of pressure. How a few simple pleasantries could have such a warming impact after days in the cooler. `Nah,` she replied, `I'm fine ...`

`Well, make sure you keep in touch.`

`I will.`

`Alright then, Cassie. Take care now.`

`Bye Andrew.`

`Bye Cassie.` His concern was unresolved as he put down the phone.

Having gathered this intel, it was time to consider what it meant. Hugo was asleep in his bedroom. With the daring of the resistance, she sat down in his favourite chair, the big bucket in the lounge that looked out across the field; the vast open space scared the hell out of the little girl but provided plenty of tranquillity to her dormant father, just as silence may need a mute button. Hugo's afternoon naps made up for sleep he lost through the night; before Lucy had fallen ill, he'd always slept well. But now, if she woke at 2am, Cassie would hear him a distance away in the kitchen turning switches and pulling levers on his grandee coffee machine, or shuffling around like a prisoner of grief, unable to settle, thinking thoughts he chose to divulge to no one, not she, not Arlene, not any of the few who may have been prepared to help. Amping up with caffeine and lurching about the place like a cave dweller did nothing for his already-lacking personality, so when he crashed, he fell deep.

Comfortable in the big chair, Cassie sat thinking about the timescale. Lucy's mobile had been disconnected for at least six weeks. The phone company could have re-used the number, putting the sim card into a new handset and selling it on to someone else. Perhaps the person who bought that phone had sent a text - using what was Lucy's old number - and by a technical snafu, it was sent to Cassie's phone as well as (or instead of) the intended recipient. Perhaps the new user was inexperienced with phones, and entered the wrong number; perhaps Cassie's number was still in the sim card, insufficiently washed by the company in between (or maybe not washed at all). Meanwhile, for sentimental reasons, the daughter hadn't been able to strike her mother's number from her phone's contacts, hence the trumpeted arrival of a misfired text under the banner of Lucy's maternal moniker.

A theory, yes. For long minutes, Cassie mused upon it, the best she could come up with. Days of thinking, of theories cast away, of reconsidering a few of the rejected, favouring some, ignoring others, a panoply of notions, yet still she could see no other half-plausible explanation. Even this theory didn't seem likely; it barely seemed possible. But she had received that text; it must have come from somewhere.

She sat back in her father's chair and sighed heavily. The lounge had been Lucy's favourite place in the house, where her family could be a family (when Hugo wasn't working and Cassie didn't have a class and she had no other commitments to attend). When the eleven-year-old had dominion, when her father had taken his gloom to the bedroom, she could recall such times far more clearly than when he was spoiling the house's temper. Now, unleashed from death's pervading literalness, her mother danced before her eyes to a record playing, boop-a-dooping at her daughter; caught by the twilight of magic hour, her long lithe body shimmered between the dusk and the night and the exotic beat of the light; reaching out to Cassie with chanteuse charm, and heavenly comic grins, pushing up her long dark hair with playful mock seductress charisma, pulling her daughter up to dance with her, the two of them swaying, boogying and bopping to the moment, to the effervescent music, the buoyancy of the confluence of fleeting intangibles, happiness with her mother a dozen miles high. She channelled these pure memories better in this room – in this chair –

than anywhere else in the house. Perhaps it was the Stonehenge of their little world, the focal point of ley lines that mattered the most, although it didn't seem to do much for Hugo, channelling whatever it was he channelled, unthinking.

Despite its mildly spooky size, the grandness of the field behind the house was never less than inspiring. Though they were close to the conurbation, the sense of space provided by this cusp of nature had once upon a time represented the having-it-of-both-ways. Privacy was provided by lines of trees along the horizon – one might as well have been in the middle of the forest, separated from the rest of the world by rows of tall oaks behind which there may be thousands of acres of primitive, prehistoric woodland, rather than the neighbour's own lavish garden. What people do in their own home, with the cool air and no one else around, how they may live as if they were the only people left on earth; how they may feel that this was their own reality, belonging to no one else. Many trees, many gardens, many worlds, many memories. Head resting side-long on the chair, Cassie stared through the window, trying to see what was close, what was far, what lived and breathed of the field; in other words, trying to see her mother.

Hugo emerged from his coma, and Arlene joined them for dinner: that is, she brought dinner, for fear of how emaciated her brother and niece would become if left to their own devices. It was a rare occasion of father and daughter sharing a meal at meal time, in the presence of a third person. Hugo and Cassie were discomfited by Arlene's arrival, unannounced, an imposition with (outwardly at least) the best of intentions. Despite her playing it cool, Arlene had recognised her niece's spirits rise during their weekend together, and was appalled to see the extent to which her bonhomie had since been corroded since by exposure to her father's gloom and the bleak atmosphere of the house. She tried to restore the good vibes, yet not all of the latent suspicion with which Cassie behaved could be attributed to Hugo; her aunt couldn't quite work out that the remainder of this unease was triggered by her own motives for being there, and in the grace notes of her behaviour: cheeky asides at Hugo's expense, references to their time away, the possibility of future trips – signs of a takeover plan? In this hostile environment, Arlene tried to curl a smile on her niece and brother's lips – but Cassie was uncommunicative with Hugo around, while he was sticking to his no-words diet. Reminiscence going back to the beginning of her recall failed to dent his perimeter.

Towards the end of the evening, Cassie's disquiet lessened enough to allow her to feel sorry for her aunt, who was trying so hard and getting so nowhere, regardless of her true motives for being here. Yet the strain of the evening started to show on her face too. Slumped in her chair, incapable of presenting a tough façade at this conflicted meal, Cassie sat up quickly, a look of alarm in her eyes. Hugo barely glanced at her, but Arlene – from whom she'd so far successfully hidden the babbles – was derailed from what she was saying by her niece's sudden movement. Cassie noticed – as she started to spout rubbish in a way that screamed "possessed" – a disorientated, disturbed look pass across her aunt's face, that moment of disgust in the uninitiated, before she suppressed that horror and stepped up to help, like the wannabe surrogate mother she was. Arlene tried to listen to the stream-of-consciousness nonsense spewing forth from Cassie's deranged lips, to defuse the babbling by a show of compassion, but as the pile of incongruity grew, she found it increasingly hard to hide how awful the demonic performance appeared to her to be.

The extent to which Hugo paid attention to his daughter's distress was confined to an undertone of irritation; he continued to eat as of nothing was happening but for the most supremely unwanted of interruptions. Looks cast in his direction for the duration of an episode – at least, for as long as he waited around – would fall upon a rumbling malevolence, a sore impatience; the eggshells on which to walk. His blinking quickening, a shortening fuse coming atop a flattened mountain of violent angst, compressed into a purity of loathing. A tick-tick-ticking time bomb. Eventually, Arlene had to move to another room, so chilling was the sight of the uncontrollable child babbling combined with the father who couldn't care less, and who may be about to detonate. Only when she heard Cassie's sobs did she go running back in, and bundle her up in her arms. Weak and vulnerable, the child welcomed this affection – hell, any affection – from wherever it came. The episodes were getting worse. Hugo dismissed himself from the pre-teen's torment, his disfavour intact; no explosion now, but no promise that there wouldn't be one.

Cassie finally calmed. Arlene asked, `What was that???` The eleven-year-old couldn't reply, shaken and dismayed. `Poor lamb,` was all her aunt said.

Arlene made it her business to come over for dinner more often, and in doing so became a veteran of the babbles. Never again did she appear to be horrified, even remotely fazed by the sight of her niece's apparent demonic possession; perhaps she wasn't, her affection able to overcome the child's deficiencies as well being enchanted by her qualities; or maybe she just hid it well. Either way, her composure was tested on numerous occasions. Sometimes during an episode her niece gripped her so tightly Arlene thought she'd be strangled, but still she didn't pull away, instead let Cassie hold on to her as hard as she needed for as long as she required.

When the babbling and sobbing stopped, her niece would sit still – often trembling – in Arlene's arms. Soothingly, her aunt would tell her more stories of Hugo as a younger man. `He wasn't always like that,` she said. `So serious, such a stick in the mud. But he was always ten years older than me, so I was always a little tyke to him, even when he met your mother and I was almost twenty. Our father died when I was six, Hugo sixteen; our mother suffered his loss just as your father is suffering over Lucy. And then, one day, mother was gone too. By this time, Hugo had met Lucy, they were already engaged. We thought he was incapable of being that way with someone, you know - being that close to her, letting Lucy get close to him - but it happened. Lord knows what he would have been like had it not been for her. Within a year of meeting they were married. Within a year of that, they had you.`

Cassie remained unmoving.

`Lucy liberated Hugo,` Arlene said. `She set him free from his seriousness. Your father laughs rarely, but, when he does, it's clear he has the same amount of mirth within him as anyone else, but it comes out on so few occasions that a year's hysteria gushes free in a room-shaking bonanza. Then, when it's run dry, he goes back into a coma. Lucy never doubted that he loved her, even if it was almost impossible for others to observe. If she could see him now, she'd know for sure.`

'Well …' said Cassie, with the bitterness only the bluntness of children can produce: 'He used up all of his love by the time he got to me.'

Arlene stroked her niece's perspirant forehead, another little hard nut in the family. 'You shouldn't be so tough on him.'

'Why not? He hates me.'

'He doesn't.'

'So why does he ignore me all the time?'

'He ignores everyone.'

'But I'm his daughter!'

'I know, honey.'

'And to be perfectly honest,' she said, 'I never meant that much to him. He was only nice to me because Mum wanted him to be. I always knew that if I was ever left alone with him, this would happen.'

'You should go a bit easier on him. He is in grief.'

And now Cassie was silent, for Arlene was making excuses for him, and if she couldn't be persuaded that Hugo detested his daughter, how could she expect Cassie to trust her on all the other stuff? They sat in silence for a few minutes, aunt letting niece brood, before Arlene said, 'I'm here to help you, darling.'

To which Cassie thought, are you sure???

In the sanctuary of her bedroom, alone and away from everyone, she continued to work on her theory of how the text message supposedly from her mother came to land in her phone. The more she pondered, the less likely it seemed she was correct to think it was an errant text sent by a new owner of the sim. This gap of good sense allowed the balloon of her longing to expand to fill the room, pregnant on the verge of exploding. Maybe her mother was out there somewhere, keeping an eye on her, close by if ever Cassie needed …

A single act of obviousness had been hunting the pre-teen from the moment the text had arrived. Terror prevented her from so doing, not of what might happen but of what might not. So far, she'd persuaded herself from thinking it was a good idea, that she'd be making herself out to be a prime idiot; even if no one else ever knew, she'd know she'd been so dumb as to think it worth trying. This knowledge would curl itself around what little confidence she had, tightening until she was denied all breath, a withered girl, not yet twelve, beaten to the floor and kicked and punched by the struggles of life, sucked free of all vitality. An ugly self-picture.

And then – a flicker: "why not?". What have you got to lose? What have you not yet lost that a simple, quick, decisive act wouldn't further take from you? But what you'd gain if …

If …

Well, there was no quantifying that.

She called up the message from "Mum".

She stared at it, though she knew every word, every character. What to say in response? How to fill her one chance at a mad act with all she wanted to express, while hedging enough to preserve some dignity if it turned out to be wrong? For there would be no second attempt should this nutty act prove to be a wretched failure. Flows of words passed through her mind with busy effusion, but nothing seemed quite right – or sane. Attempts discarded, drafts turned upside down and backwards, delaying her from the act, the contemplation of which generated an all-over body-fear that made her wonder if she could stand the strain. If she couldn't endure this, how would she be able to make her way through life?

After several hours, Cassie had exhausted herself with nothing to show for it. She lay back in bed, breathing heavy with anxiety.

`This is stupid,` she hissed, and in a single, fluid motion, sat up, grabbed her phone, typed, "Mum, is that you? xx" and sent the text to the mysterious correspondent before chucking it in the drawer so she wouldn't be able to hear if and when the triple tone announced the arrival of a text from ...

4

Andrew Faro was sitting at his desk, thinking about heading home. It was just after six, and there was nothing going on, his office untroubled by the day. But just as he was about to stand, his phone began to buzz. He answered, and was told by his PA that a client had arrived, wanting to see him. Faro sighed, asked who it was. The name came as a surprise, and a few moments later, Hugo was sitting in his office.

Ever hospitable, the lawyer said, `Can I get you coffee?`

Hugo shook his head.

`Okay, then!` Faro replied, settling down for this most unusual visit. `What's up?`

The silent widower had spoken so little in the months since Lucy had died that he was clearly out of practice when it came to communicating with others. Faro could see he had no one else to turn to. He gave him room and the time to find the means by which to express himself.

`I had this ... strange thing happen,` Hugo finally began, his voice soft, wavering, broken from lack of use. `And I need to ... talk to someone about it.`

`I'm honoured that you came to me. Please, tell me what's on your mind.`

The widower chose his words carefully ... slowly ... with an effort excruciating for the listener as well as the speaker. `This is going to sound ... random but, but I ... have always been a book man. I have ... taken great comfort in ... in books. Much more so than ... from people ... who can be ... vain ... unreliable ... cruel. Well, so I ... collect books.`

`Yes,` said Faro. `I remember the tour Lucy gave me of your house when you moved in, how there was one big room teeming with ... all kinds of ...`

Hugo nodded. `Not long before Lucy and I ... Lucy and I got married, we ... went to Australia. I had never ... been; Lucy wanted to go. It seemed like such a long way ...`

`It is,` the lawyer said, warmly. `It's even further when your client's not paying.` He smiled; Hugo did not. Faro didn't take it personally. He let the widower continue.

`We were there for ... three weeks,` Hugo explained, in halting, incremental fashion. `I had already asked her to ... marry me; she had already ... said ... said yes. The wedding was quite ... soon, much of it already ... already sorted. Mother had died and I ... needed ... a break from work, from mourning, from ... myself. Lucy ... as always ... came up with the idea. So ... off we went. I never had ... any doubts at all that ... that she was the one for ... for me. And on that ... holiday ... we just ... we just got even ... closer. We did whatever ... she wanted to do. We went along ... along the east coast ... And while we ... while we were there, in

Australia, I ... I carried on buying books at ... my usual rate, and reading them while ... Lucy would be on the phone, or we were ... on the beach or ... while she was getting ready for ... us to go out. When ... it was ... time for us ... to ... come home, I had almost twenty and it just seemed ... silly to fly them all the way back ... with us. A boxful. So I ... I took them into ... this ... little second ... second hand book store near where we'd ... been staying towards the end of our time there. I'd ... even bought a few from this same shop so ... so ... so it felt like I'd rented them ... rather than ... rather than bought them. The owner of the store was ... happy, grateful ... and that was that.`

Hugo paused, the dredging of these memories a piercing agony. His face, in stasis, as if he were right back there with Lucy, and she was still alive.

`Which is why you're here?` Faro said, the significance of his client's tale as yet beyond him, and keen to get out of the office some time this evening.

`But that ... wasn't that,` Hugo continued, barely enough life flickering back into his face for him to speak. `To this day there's still, there's still ... not much I find more ... soothing than walking into a bookshop, and browsing. It's ... a form of relaxation for me. It's where I go to ... to ... to escape from it all. So I've been doing a ... a lot of browsing in bookshops these last few months. When I ... when I cannot take being cooped up ... in the house ... any longer ... when there are no more ... ways I can think about all I've lost and all I'll never have again and ... and ... and when I feel that the less Cassie sees of me ... the better ... the happier ... the less scarred by this she'll ... be.`

`You do realise what a great kid you've got there, don't you?`

The widower blinked a couple of times; Andrew couldn't tell if the message penetrated his shell; it seemed not to, for Hugo was continuing his faltering raison d'être. `Through book shops I've walked for hours and hours, trying just ... to let go ... to let go of ... these memories ... like that trip with her ... like so much of our time together ... to fool myself into thinking that I never had a wife. If I had no wife then I ... I couldn't have lost my wife ... and I wouldn't have to feel like this. I walk through book shops and I ... browse the shelves and ... I am someone else. I'm ... not who ... who I was when I ... came into ... the shop and ... I don't ever have to be that man again until ... I ... I leave. And so I buy dozens of books and ... and ...`

Hugo came to a halt. Faro could see he was trembling, and may need a little less office and a little more encouragement to expunge what he'd come here to say. `Listen,` the lawyer said, `I've been stuck in this cell all day. You know my favourite watering hole? Why don't we go there for a drink?`

Hugo looked at him with a haunted expression that screamed out: people.

`Trust me,` Faro said. `We'll have all the privacy we need.`

And so, ten minutes later, they were settled in a remote booth in a bar across the road from the office. The lawyer had in front of him a whiskey, while Hugo's own glass of still water sat with the abundant expectation of not being touched.

Faro encouraged the widower to continue. Hugo did so faltering as before. `Amongst the places I've been to ... to buy books, I was ... browsing ... through a shop I ... know well. It's five ... five minutes from where I live. And I saw this book. You know ... how sometimes in shops or ... libraries you're ... you're drawn to a book you've already read although ... you don't realise ... realise this until you've got ... closer ... to ... it? What's attracting you now is the ... is the same thing that attracted you the first time. The cover ... or the title ... or the ... kind of edition it is or ... it could be anything. And there's this mild ... disappointment when you realise you've already ... read it, that you ... already ... already enjoyed reading it for the first time. You wish you'd never seen it before, you wish you'd never been ... seduced by it ... in the past ... so that ... you could have that pleasure now.`

Hugo paused. Faro drew heavily on his whiskey. They could both hear the darkness drawing in closely around them.

`I ... I walked towards it, towards this ... book as it sat ... as it sat ... as it sat on the shelf, in the shop five ... five minutes from ... from where I ... live ... and in that moment I realised that I had read it before, I had once owned a copy of that ... edition, exactly like ... the one on the shelf, right there. As I do when ... I'm drawn to a ... to a book I've been drawn to in the past ... I picked it off the shelf, held it like I was ... shaking its hand, like I ... was saying hello to a friend I hadn't ... seen ... in a long time.`

Faro took a long strike of liquor.

`So I'm holding this book in my ... hands, just ... a week ago ... and it's a ... a paperback I ... enjoyed when I was ... in Australia with Lucy, twelve, thirteen years past. I remembered the story ... and this edition too. It was not a great book. It was an entertainment, nothing ... nothing more than that ... no great ... work of literature ... but ... I ... enjoyed it. And the way the book ... felt, the paper immaculate, there was integrity in its weight in my hands though it was not a ... not a big book, not a long book, not a book you'd pick up in an ... airport or anything special that you could ... you could put ... in your ... inside pocket and walk around or sit in a cafe and read it there or ... stand on ... a train with it and look ... super smart. It was just ... you know ... an easy read. I liked this book: what it was, how it felt, how it smelt. And then suddenly I realised ... that I had once owned not just another copy of an identical edition but this very copy.`

Hugo looked up at Faro; his face had changed – the widower of hope. The lawyer's warm indulgence dissolved into his whiskey, the second of which was on its way. He'd come to let his long-standing client break his Garbo silence, hence his desire for a little comfort while hand-holding. But he should have known Hugo better: he was serious, and now they were getting to the nub of it, Faro would admit to the onset of that sinking feeling.

Hugo nodded. `I had owned this very book when I was in Australia with Lucy. It was in the box I had taken into the second hand book store before we came home.`

Faro's second whiskey arrived just in time. He thanked the waitress and took a long glug, watchful of his client. He smiled and said, `Come now, my friend, I mean ...`

There was an awkward pause.

Faro realised he was committed by his sceptical tone and had to speak his mind. `Twelve years? From Australia? Hugo, it's not the same book!`

The point he knew was coming, the point he'd been waiting for. The widower said, steadily in his faltering way, `So there I am, standing in the book shop, flicking ... through a novel I had once enjoyed on holiday with Lucy in Australia. More than ten years ago. Without … realising it, I came to page 96, and my heart almost stopped.`

Hugo paused, his expression suddenly more animated than Faro could recall, even in the happiest of times when all was fine. He held it for as long as it took. The lawyer nodded: tell me what you saw.

`Lipstick,` Hugo said.

`Lipstick …?` Faro echoed.

`Lipstick,` Hugo explained.

Faro channelled more whiskey down his throat.

`At our hotel in Sydney,` the widower continued, `Where we spent our last week in Australia, we stayed in room 96. When it was time to go home, and I was piling up the books to take to the second hand store, Lucy opened each one and planted a big kiss on that page, page 96. She knew it would drive me crazy – I hate it when books are defaced – but how could I object? She was a romantic, but I … don't think she did anything that … struck me as more my kind of romantic while we were together. She freshened her lipstick after each book, and signed every one of them in her own way, on page 96.`

Faro sat in silence.

`So when I saw the faded lipstick mark on page 96 of the book I was holding in a second hand book shop five minutes from where I live just one week ago, that's how I knew it was the same copy I had read in Australia more than a decade past. I ran to the checkout to buy it and left the shop feeling like I was smuggling a criminal out of the country. When I got home, I looked at the book again, to make sure I wasn't going crazy. It was her lipstick, Andrew, it was Lucy!`

Faro sat for a few moments, mulling over what he'd been told. Then he said, `You ... unh ... you really want me to respond, Hugo?`

`Lucy has sent me this book.`

`Hugo ...`

`She's trying to contact me!`

`Assuming the book is the same one ...`

`It is!`

`So it's travelled ten thousand miles over a period of more than a decade???`

`Why should I find it now?`

`Why indeed?`

`Because Lucy has sent it to me now.`

`No, Hugo ...`

`It's a message.`

`It's a coincidence.`

`She's trying to contact me.`

`No ...`

`But you yourself are saying: should I assume that it's only arrived now, after travelling for more than ten years around the world?`

`Compared to the alternative? Hugo, no. It's a coincidence.`

`How do you know?`

`Because it's impossible.`

`How can you say that?`

`Because I'm not the one in mourning.`

A grimace of pain passed across the widower's face. Faro spoke more frankly than he might have done had he not sunk two tasty whiskeys. Though he felt sorry for his client, such incisive commentary was clearly required were Hugo not to go jumping off the deep end. Still, perhaps a corrective was in order. `You've just lost your wife. God knows what that must be like; I don't. But it's times like these when you need people to keep you on the right side of the street. Your brain's gonna be all over the place, not to mention your emotions, and I will do whatever I can to help but, but you have to listen to me when I say; thinking something like this ... It's just not gonna do you any good.`

Hugo sat, his face cast in shadow by the booth and by Faro. He was silent again, sure to be thinking hostile thoughts about the lawyer's so-called advice, about the lawyer himself. `You've known me for twenty years, Andrew,` he said, when it appeared to Faro that the mental voodoo doll had been well and truly spiked. `When have I ever said anything that would make you think I was crazy?`

The lawyer said, `You never lost your wife before to cancer.`

`But it was her lipstick! It was her kiss. All the way from Australia? And if you don't believe me, I'll show you the book!`

`It's not a case of me not believing you ...`

`So what's your problem?`

`You're asking me to accept that …`

`She's reaching out to me! I don't know what to do, what am I supposed to do? I've been trying to work it out, but I don't know where to begin.`

`Hugo,` Faro said, looking at him firmly, `Lucy is not trying to contact you.`

`So explain it. Explain how the book got here, let alone that it should arrive now. There were twenty books, Andrew, she kissed every one of them, every one on page 96, and that was more than ten years ago on the other side of the world. Explain it to me!`

`I already did.`

`It's not a coincidence.`

`It is.`

`I don't believe in coincidence.`

`Well I do. I've seen it happen far more times than I'd care to consider. It's a form of luck, so if you want an explanation, there you go. Perhaps this really is the book Lucy kissed and which you took to a shop in Australia, and it really has taken all that time to make its way back. So you're lucky it's returned to you now, you're lucky that this memory has arrived, a memory of the most romantic time you had with the only woman you ever loved. But it's nothing more than luck, Hugo. The reason you can't work out what to do about it is because there's nothing to do, there's nothing you can do.`

By now, Hugo had sat back in his chair, retreating into his comatose state.

`Do you want to know what I think?` Faro said.

The widower didn't reply.

`Well, I'll tell you anyway. I think you should to forget all about this book and start talking to that daughter of yours, so she realises she hasn't lost both of her parents. She's a great kid, Hugo, but the only way to honour Lucy now is by helping Cassie cope with this tragedy. And in doing so maybe you'll come to terms with the fact that she really is gone, and nothing's going to change that, however much you might wish it weren't so.`

He sat at home, in the dark. The house was silent; past 2am. Cassie had long since gone to bed. Arlene – staying the night – had waited for her brother to return from wherever it was he'd gone without saying, to make sure he was okay. He'd come back in a mood indistinguishable from the bleak demeanour he'd inhabited for months, not so far removed from his usual excessive seriousness. But she could tell that he had taken a few extra knocks tonight, that he must have been tormenting himself in some unknown fashion, and though she may ask him about his evening, to be of aid, of comfort, she knew he wouldn't tell her anything. She sat with him for a few minutes, scanning him over; he could feel her penetrating gaze – and then hear the dull thud as she struck the concrete that would prevent her from penetrating any further. She shook her head, just as she did when they were younger. He'd made himself a venomously strong-looking espresso before settling into his chair in the lounge, to look out over the field that at night became a sea, an ocean, a void. And then she too had gone to bed, leaving Mr Happy alone to brood.

Only now did he realise how conducive his house was to heavy introspection, an amplifier of the dominant emotion reverberating within. The removal of Lucy had altered the dynamic of walls and ceilings and floors that had moved not a millimetre nor changed their style since she'd died. The field at the back of the house: so romantic to his wife, who shimmered in the sunlight that came flooding in, and who could have danced her way across the wilds in crepuscular sunrise. But she was gone, and the sunlight too. Instead, a full moon petrified the darkness of the field, the cusp vanished into the distance, beyond which terrifying expressions of fundamental fear lurked. The light that crept through the windows lay its long sheet over this territory, opening a valley through which every nightmare hallucination could rush, made real.

Faro was wrong, he said to himself, sunk deep into a chair near-consumed by the encroaching moonlight, the advancing hordes. He could have taken umbrage at the way his supposed friend had spoken to him: casting the notion out of hand. Yet bitterness belonged elsewhere: Faro was not possessed of all of the facts, so what else could you expect from a lawyer? That Hugo hadn't finished telling him all he'd gone there to say explained the hole in Faro's understanding; after the last gruesome phase in his life, he was getting used to people talking to him as if he were (a) a child or (b) a vast swathe of tragedy encased in human skin, both of which provided others with ample opportunity to condescend. Hugo had been willing to provide the missing piece of evidence, but with the lawyer in a disparaging mood, Hugo was avowed of what he knew before he went in: that some things are beyond the understanding of those who are not directly affected. Perhaps Faro would have laughed more had Hugo provided this key fact, helped by his whiskeys. He didn't get the chance. Hugo didn't have enough memories of Lucy to allow his precious few mementos to be ridiculed. But he was convinced, even if Faro was not.

For a conversation had taken place between the couple many years ago. Despite his wife's hunger for travel, one of his many aching regrets was that he failed to indulge this desire often enough. He earnt well and she was wealthy, so it was not a matter of means, rather attitude. On the topic she had deferred to him, and in his redoubtable seriousness, he'd stayed close to the office, to the desk. Yet every now and then they did manage to escape the tractor beam of commerce. The missing evidence he didn't have the chance (or will) to reveal to Faro was a memorable moment in a blissful trip. He and Lucy were in the South of France, walking through a harbour near their hotel, having eaten of a heavenly meal in a sumptuous restaurant which overlooked yachts and the distant horizon, the sun slowly setting in the sea, and with a couple of glasses of wine and the warm evening air, as they ambled towards a bar that served whatever cocktail you could think to ask for, Lucy had her arm hooked in his, and they had been chatting all evening about serious stuff, about the effervescent nothing, and then, from nowhere, she'd said, a slightly naughty, slightly drunken smile in her voice, `Will you make me a promise?`

He was tickled by her tone, and in a rare mood to tease, he replied: `I can't do that until you tell me what it is.`

She appreciated the play, and nuzzled in. `I want you to promise me that ... if you die, you'll find a way to contact me.`

Hugo was charmed indeed. `I promise.`

`But not in any scary, freak-me-out kind of way – do it in a manner that'll impress the hell out of me. Do it gently, so I won't die of fright. Do it in a way that I'll know for sure that it's you, that it couldn't be anyone else. Do it in a way that's romantic.`

`I promise,` he said. `But on one condition.`

`Oh? And what might that be?!`

`That you promise the same to me.`

`Okay, Mr Wheeler Dealer, I promise!`

A simple aside, nothing more than that. They had walked on, enjoyed their creative cocktails, the rest of the evening, and that rare holiday; most of all, they had enjoyed each other. And now, a catastrophe later, as Hugo sat in the chair in his lounge in which the moon reach merged with the petrified field, he had no doubt that she'd honoured her side of the bargain, that she had kept her promise and contacted him from the great beyond in a manner as gentle and romantic as it was unarguable. He needed no further proof. But how can one say that to a lawyer?

He stood from his chair, his lair, and walked to the kitchen. Again, a Lucy creation – the whole house her style, her concept, furnished to her taste, finished to her liking. He ricocheted at the decisions she'd made in every table top, every work surface, every cupboard handle, every one a reminder of what he'd lost. In the kitchen, his only contribution: the coffee machine to which he returned so many times a day. His sole confidante, the one entity in the house that heard his unspoken confession. He stared at it now, its gleam faded. Bespoke and engineered to perfection, he made himself yet another nocturnal espresso, enemy of sleep. Unable to catch more than three hours in a session since Lucy's diagnosis, he was now on a body rhythm that knew of no human land, with no guide through this unfamiliar territory of long caffeine shadows and Dali-esque twists of night. Though it may not aid his sleep, the coffee was a boon to brooding, making it the only tactile facility he appeared still to have. With expert barista skill, a hot espresso was soon in a tiny Lucy-chosen cup held taut. He drank it quick, cued another, and returned to his moonlit chair.

He had to concede that Faro had at least one valid point. Only after Lucy died did he realise how few mementos he had of her. Sure, the house, the lifestyle – but they were monuments, not the echoes of private moments that, taken together, define and describe a relationship. She'd only been dead for three months and already he was finding it hard to remember how she felt, her voice when they were laying in bed together, how she tilted her head when she laughed, how she could mimic virtually anyone. He was ashamed at being so disloyal – you said you loved her, how could you forget her so quickly? But the mind was callous, the cells turn over and bury the past, it's harder to see, to feel, to hear. So the lawyer had been accurate in identifying his good fortune at having the lipstick book, regardless of where it came from. He hadn't dismissed the fact that it was the volume Lucy had kissed way back when, that he was the recipient of so specific a memory that he could recall her as she layered on the rouge, puckered up for show and then marked page 96 in each of the tomes in that box for ever more. Every time he looked at that page, every time he picked up the volume – he only need think of it and there she was again, conjured up in full-flesh recollection inspired by that well-travelled digest. With so few memories, it stood like a beacon, illuminating the road back to her.

Perhaps there was a shade of guilt in Lucy's gift. When she was dying, she'd allowed herself to be commandeered by Cassie. He let it happen, to the extent that he had no choice: he let Lucy use the little time she had in the manner she felt most appropriate, which meant giving it all to their daughter. He vanished into his work. It felt like the right thing to do – and was clearly what Lucy wanted. But the right thing to do done can often corrode in retrospect, as time passes, as people pass. Once upon a time his wife wouldn't have forsaken him – but for Cassie she did, and Hugo could see when he looked at the eleven-year-old the thief of his last months with his dying soul mate. There was so much he'd wanted to say to Lucy, and he was the kind of person who needed a lot of time to say it, to bring it from so deep from within. So many things he'd wanted them to do – the ski-ing trips, the bottles of wine, the fine steaks, the long sandy beaches, the spindly streets of Old Europe, the wide boulevards of the New World ... Just say thanks, for providing him with a bridge to the rest of the world, for acknowledging, understanding and catering for feelings that no one else ever bothered with. Now he was stranded back on the same small island onto which he'd been born, where it was assumed he was a mechanical device utilised only for the purpose of work, with no hungers, no needs, no dreams of his own, and nothing left to take him any closer to Lucy.

Cassie had a mountain of memories. He knew in her bedroom she had hundreds of hours of footage of she and Lucy together. It was wrong, unfair, blah blah blah, but he was feverishly jealous of this hoard. He'd coveted nothing in his life until now, inescapably resentful as he was of her collection of Lucy fragments. This was no starter jealousy, no jealousy for beginners: this was a furious, despairing sense of theft, with the booty not only taken but stored under his own roof, right under his nose. A glowing as malignant as Lucy's cancer came from Cassie's bedroom every time she opened the door. Contained in there: the only true record of the woman his wife had been. As the chemo robbed her hair, and Lucy had taken to wearing headscarves and bandannas, in Cassie's footage, he'd see the passing of time – and the ever-nearing closeness of death – in the change of this headwear, but he'd also be able to watch footage in reverse-chronological order, and indulge in the illusion of her return to good health. That may help, but he wouldn't know, for Cassie had eaten greedily of her mother's dying time, and in the background of those hundreds of hours you'd barely see the father struggling to contain his own needs.

Hugo despised this taste of bitterness; he drank espressos to halt its corrosion. Lucy went quicker than expected, and by expected they meant hoped. Terminal cancer placed her in a box the moment they were told of the diagnosis, and from then on it was an untidy race, full of disarray, arms flapping, panic stations, no-one really knew what was going on, and how can one prioritise a dying person's time? They had tried, like every family in that circumstance, but they'd got it wrong, to his cost, and he was no longer capable of resisting the shoves of his emotions, and the rage towards his daughter which was getting no better, only worse. Cassie was such a clever girl, so sensitive and perceptive, that she couldn't help but detect the extent and direction of her father's resentment, though she was as much of a victim of this tragedy as he, and they really should have been in it together, yet couldn't be further apart.

He walked through the house, to stroll off the coffee, but the caffeine wasn't what kept him from sleep, it was thoughts of the two women in his life. His sister came and went with no notion of responsibility, wholly unreliable, a little fantasist. She'd made a complete mess or her life and now, with nothing better to do, seemed intent on making a nuisance in his. She was trying to ingratiate herself with Cassie, form a united front against him – she'd recognised what a willing little partner she'd have in that venture, the last thing either father or daughter needed – same old Arlene. With most siblings, age gaps fade into irrelevance as they get older; the decade between his younger sister and he seemed to expand; she was still in effect a child – unmarried, no kids – and he was an old man, a widower. She appeared to be living a fantasy of family coming together in a crisis, but she'd always been a pushy little thing, and now she was trying to push her way into a situation that required no further complication, no extra interpretation.

He couldn't keep her from just dropping by. Another evening, another disaster. With Cassie gone to bed, Arlene cornered him with a cup of what she knew was his favourite coffee. `Can we talk?`

He did not reply.

`Well, I can talk,` she said. `And you can listen, if nothing else. You have a daughter.`

He remained impassive.

`You know,` she continued, `That eleven-year-old girl you sometimes see walking about the house babbling like a loon? The little girl who's just lost her mother, but still needs her father? I'm sure you'd recognised her: if you look at her face, you'll notice she looks a hell of a lot like you.`

He finally turned his gaze on her.

`Ah, there you are!` she said. `And I thought I was talking to a coma victim. You're the walking dead, Hugo. You could drink all of the coffee in Colombia and it still won't shake you from the doldrums. You need help. Let me help.`

He stared at her.

`Is that all you're gonna do?` she said.

He started to walk past her, but she blocked him off. He glowered, she glowered back. He tried to walk around her but she stopped him again. So annoying. He was getting angry, Arlene could tell: the way he lowered his gaze, the stillness of his jaw.

When he was younger, she knew that when he behaved this way, he was trying to disappear completely. To the unknowing, it was an act of intimidation. `When Lucy died, did you take a vow of silence?` she asked.

And then finally he looked up. Arlene could see the emptiness inside him, the decay, as if someone had cast acid across his entrails, and the slow fizz inside had carved out all that lay within, and there was nothing left of the man she'd known for all these years, or even the boy she once knew in the past.

6

When Cassie woke each morning, before doing anything else, she checked her phone for texts from her mother. She'd reset her ring tone so messages from others would sing a different tune from Lucy's triple-tone – she'd know the moment the text arrived that it was from her! Even so, during the day, she never went more than an hour without quadruple-checking, an imploration to the long-distance lost mother echoing through the boundaries of mortality. She was alone in the house – her father unreachable, her aunt untrusted – but only in the human sense; physically they were nearby, along with their agendas. Cassie would have to contain the tornado of emotion a second text from "Mum" would unleash. Hugo wouldn't even notice, but Arlene would sense in a flash that ... that ...

Well, what? What would it be like if there was a second text, if it did come from Lucy? She might think she was going mad – she might be right. Witnesses of her babbling may say she'd already caved under the twin pressures: the actual loss of her mother and the effective loss of her father. But now there would be proof: she'd have two texts, making it clear the first one wasn't just sent to someone else and received by Cassie by mistake or for inexplicable technical reasons. The odds of the same bizarre delivery happening twice were so extreme as to be non-existent. Meanwhile, there had as yet been no response from a new possible owner of the number that belonged to Lucy. Surely that person would have replied to her message of Mum, is that you? xx, realising that they'd sent the preceding text to the wrong person by mistake, and acknowledge this by sending another, clarifying the matter and apologising for the error? The implication of this evidence could only be that the texts were meant for her. So it would only be a matter of time before Lucy replied, and Cassie would respond – and they would be talking again! Until then, she kept on watching her phone for sudden illumination, and listening out for the triple-tone announcing her mother's return.

Mid-morning, she'd notched up an appetite, having skipped breakfast; she hadn't made herself any – nor had anyone else. Arlene was coming over later to cook dinner, but empty hungry hours loomed ahead. In a parallel universe, she could have run to her father and ask that he take her out for the day; they could jump into his car and drive wherever she wanted to go, wherever he thought she may like. But Cassie knew her feet were planted in this universe, and rather than running to Hugo, planned to stay as far away from him as possible. To achieve that peaceful if pathetic outcome, she intended to open the door to her bedroom, go to the kitchen, get some food and return to the safety of her private chamber without so much as seeing his shadow from the corners of her eyes. She hovered by her door, keen to escape, but too much pressure came from the other side, from the remainder of the house. She stumbled back on to her bed, starving.

She crossed her fingers that Arlene would call, her aunt perceptive (or sneaky) enough to divine these lunch time vibes and come to her aid. Cassie had spent hours mulling over Arlene's true motives, for so often she seemed genuine, but even after finishing with that ungainful pursuit, she was still stuck in her bedroom, hungry and trapped in a large, murky house, in the corners of which dwelt her father's Cassie Hatred. She might try to escape him and his loathing, but he'd laid bombs of repugnance wherever she may trek, making it impossible for her to be comfortable anywhere but her bedroom. Out in the open, he'd hold her responsible for Lucy's death, saving his severest moods for when she needed him the most. It wasn't just the intimidation of his coma-like silence. When they were alone in the house, Cassie was terrified that wordless, inert, vanished Hugo would suddenly snap. Just as once upon a happier time he'd be so serious and then a year would pass and all his joy would come flooding out, she was terrified now that, instead of joy, a mass of poison, invective, disgust would erupt from his frozen exterior, the scowl breached by the contained uncontainable at last breaking free, upsurging in her direction. The less she saw him, the less likely it was to happen. In her room she only had to fear the knock at the door, and could pretend to sleep, or listen to music. But in the realm of the house, where every nook and cranny had been turned against her, she knew she was taking her chances.

Hunger pangs finally forced her to risk it. Possessing a private salle de bains was not enough – she ought to stash up on supplies: tins, chocolate, orange juice: provisions for survival if not the complexion. Cassie listened to the immediate outside to make sure he wasn't prowling nearby. Slowly, she opened her bedroom door, stepping out into the short hall that led to the landing, where Hugo's bedroom could be found, along with the guest rooms. Soundlessly, she moved along, listening for her father as a prey listens for the hunter. She reached the landing and the pinnacle of the extravagant staircase. Each step down seemed to betray her, the softest echo into the wide expanse of the ground level hall a clarion to her vengeful father. She made it to ground level without being seen, or heard; the air febrile with menace. She looked into the lounge. Blood pumped through her head so heavy it was painful: Hugo's arm was hanging from the side of the chair. He was posited within, napping after an all night morbidathon. She took no chances, moved to the kitchen as silently as she arrived. A flurry of eggs and milk, salt and pepper, some grated cheese and olive oil in the pan; a couple of hunks of the French bread Arlene brought last night (zapped in the oven to soften it up), hefty slides of butter; a long cool glass of milk, a tray, and every ten seconds a glance through to the wide open lounge and her father's unmoving arm in the chair. An omelette, as good as would be found in any decent cafe, a heap of chocolate, the utensils in the dishwasher, and if the smell woke Hugo, it no longer mattered for she'd be back in her room, closing the door, sealing herself inside, and more fool him. Safe in her lair, eating with relief, she was out of the way of his revulsion.

And yet before she knew what was happening, she was once again seated at the dinner table and there he was, in all of his malevolent iciness. Not so deft after all, for there was always a later occasion, always another time, and she was again subject to that pain-inflicting scowl, that long-lingering silent accusation. Arlene divined an extremely good meal and lavished attention on her comatose brother and neurotic niece with the dedication / determination of a righteous nun in a leper colony. But her efforts were to no effect. Hugo had come to a complete halt. He didn't speak, smile; he barely looked at the others at the table. The Medusa gaze contaminated everything around him: Cassie, Arlene, the house, the field. Tonight his gloom was destructive, a bully of a mood; the bricks and glue of their abode nervy, an incorrect tone may fracture the structure holding up the roof, the once-happy home shattering around them, and they'd be cut apart by the downfall of shards of glass, pummelled by splintering masonry, buried alive beyond rescue. Wilting, the little girl felt littler and littler, so tiny her father may cough and she'd vanish. He didn't care for her obvious distress, and Arlene could do nothing about it. Doomed to endure a dinner she couldn't swallow, Cassie's anxiety was amplified by a certainty that if she tried to gulp, she'd vomit her soul and lungs and guts and that really would be the end of her.

Arlene also struggled with the unrelenting stress, her head tilting back and forth between Cassie and Hugo. The only one making conversation, eventually she gave up and endured the subsequent long silences, the drone of dead time piling up. She too lost her appetite, could summon no more banter, raconteur no further anecdotes, no CPR to enliven the conversation. The acid of Hugo's corrosion fizzed away at the table top, the fridge, everything on which they sat – it wouldn't have surprised her if they suddenly dropped to the floor, their chairs dissolved beneath them. She smiled at the notion, especially if it happened in unison, but her grin was quickly captured and shot to death, and she remained a morose participant of this ongoing wake. Her eyes on Cassie, she wanted to take the poor girl away from this hell hole for ever.

`IoncereadabouttheSuezCanal ...` the eleven-year-old said. As soon as she did, her eyes hollowed out with anxiety. `Itwasareallyinterestingthing,` she continued, brutally against her will. Arlene watched with sad, careworn eyes; as if the poor girl was not suffering enough, her babbles would present Hugo with a wide-angled opportunity to glower, to glare, to insinuate, to punish, to let know about all she knew already. Cassie expounded upon the Suez Crisis. Facts spilled from her mouth, on the point but disjointed, rapid, blurting neatly. Her inability to stop talking was directly proportionate to her fear of the eruption her babbling might provoke. Aunt's methods of dealing with niece had drastically improved; she intervened lest things get worse before they get better.

`Come on, honey,` Arlene said. `Breathe ...`

`AnthonyEdenhadbeensuchapromisingprimemini steronceupon ...`

`Grab the words with each breath you take ...`

`AtatimeofintensemistrustintheMiddleEast ...`

Arlene stood up to calm her down, to help her defeat an attack skewed atop an unhappy day of slow-baking tension. The eyes of her niece were fixed on Hugo, who acknowledged nothing. Arlene saw how fearful she was of her father – how terrified she'd become of him.

`PresidentNasserhadseenhisopportunityto ...`

`You can do it,` Arlene said. `Breathe, come on now, breathe, deeply!`

`ThegenerallyheldviewisthatEdenseriouslymiscalc
ulatedwhen …`

`Get your breathing under control …`

`Butthereweretoomanypoliticalinterestsintheregio
nandtoomanypowerfulplayerswhowerekeptoutofthel
oopmuchtotheir …`

`Catch it, Cassie, don't let it run away with you,
catch it, catch it and hold it!`

`AndtheMaryCeleste,` she said, leaping subjects.
`AshipthatsailedoutofParrsboroNovaScotia …`

`Focus on the words …`

`Ashipwhichwasontheafternoonof4December187
2foundadriftwithnooneonboardandnoapparentreaso
nforthecrewhavingabandonedship …`

`Eat them up, Cassie, eat those words!`

`Therehadbeennosignofabattleoranemergency …`

`Eat them up and spit them out!`

`Itwasasifeveryonehadjustdecidedtowalkoffintoth
emiddleoftheoceanandnever …`

` W W W W W I I I I L L L L L
Y Y Y Y Y Y Y Y Y O O O O O U U U U U
S S S S H H H H U U U U U U T T T T
UUUUUUUPPPPPPP.`

His voice drove a steam engine through the room.
Arlene halted. Her gaze swivelled. Cassie babbled.
She couldn't stop. The words spilled at breakneck
pace. Her eyes widening, for here it came. Hugo's
face turned downwards. His chin set to kill. Scarlett

infused an exhale of silence. The background hum, babbling a prayer for peace. And then it began.

`What are you talking about?` he screamed. `Why are you making so much racket? WHAT ARE YOU SAYING, YOU STUPID CHILD? WHY DON'T YOU JUST SHUT UP? I DON'T want to sit here and listen to you talking such rubbish.`

`... nevertellanyonewheretheyweregoingbut ...`

`Shut up, you insane little beast,` he yelped. `You sicken me with your horrible ways, you lurk about this house like you think I don't notice but I hear every move you make, I SEE YOU, I wish you'd disappear so I'd never have to see you again ...`

`Hugo, what are you ...` Arlene said.

`BUT YOU'RE HERE,` he continued, `EVERYWHERE I TURN, I MOVE AROUND THE HOUSE, YOU'RE HERE, BABBLING, AND YET STILL YOU LOOK AT ME AS IF I AM THE ONE WHO'S MAD.`

`Therehadbeennopreviousproblemsswiththe ...`

`YOU'RE HAUNTING ME, I CAN'T GET AWAY FROM YOU ...`

Tears were rolling down Cassie's humiliated face.
` ... andnoonehaseverbeenabletoexplainwhat ...`

`That I LOST LUCY BUT I AM STUCK WITH YOU???`

`Hugo, stop.`

`THAT I HAVE TO ENDURE THIS LIFE???`

`Hugo, enough!`

`Therehavebeenmanyrumoursandtheoriesbut ...`

`THAT YOU TOOK ALL OF LUCY'S TIME WHEN SHE WAS DYING, YOU SELFISH, DISGUSTING, ABYSMAL, LITTLE BRAT.`

Arlene yelled, `HUGO, SHUT UP.`

He fully turned to his sobbing daughter, seemingly determined that if her mother lived no longer then neither should she. `YOU TOOK LUCY FROM ME,` he screamed, banging the table to punctuate his fury. `YOU'RE THE REASON I HAVE NOTHING LEFT. SHE WAS THE ONLY THING IN MY LIFE, AND NOW I CAN'T SEE HER, I CAN'T HEAR HER, I CAN'T REMEMBER WHO SHE WAS AND THAT'S ALL BECAUSE OF YOU.`

`HUGO!` Arlene screamed.

`Arumourneversubstantiatedfocusedononeofthesa ilors ...` Cassie babbled, her weeping peaking.

`YOU SPOUT THIS RUBBISH,` he roared. `THIS NON-STOP BILGE ABOUT ANYTHING AND NOTHING AT ALL. YOU MAKE ME WANT TO SCREAM WHEN YOU START AND WHEN YOU KEEP ON GOING. YOU DON'T TALK ABOUT ANYTHING, AND WHEN I SEE YOU ALL I CAN THINK OF IS THAT ANY TIME NOW, ANY TIME, HERE IT COMES, SHE'S GOING TO START, AND THE AIRWAVES AROUND ME ARE GOING TO BE POLLUTED ONCE MORE.`

`HUGO, YOU UNCONSCIONABLE BULLY, LEAVE HER ALONE.`

`Arumourthatasailorsentamessagebacktohisloved onebywritingacodeinacopyofabookthatfounditswayt oheralmostfouryearslater ...`

He stopped as suddenly as he'd started, a car crashed into a wall. He stared at his howling daughter, his eyes open so wide they looked as if they were about to pop. The house continued to vibrate with his rage as the screaming of his shouting dissipated into the walls; he played Cassie's last sentence over and over again in his head.

`HUGO, YOU MONSTER,` Arlene screamed. `I HOPE YOU'RE PLEASED, YOU SHOULD BE THE ONE THAT DIED, YOU'RE DEAD INSIDE ALREADY.`

She took Cassie's hand and led her rushing from the room. A bundle of exhaustion, tears and anxiety, the eleven-year-old went with her gladly. Hugo watched insofar as he could see anything other than those words, the words that had just come babbling from his daughter's mouth, words about the rumour of a code in a book that found its way to a loved one across unimaginable boundaries of space and time.

7

Cassie lay on her bed, sobbing, shaking, the episode over but feeling destroyed. Arlene lay next to her, holding her close, whispering it would be okay, she'd be alright, calm down, relax, breathe and forget all about her hideous father. Aunt promised niece that tomorrow she'd take her away for a few days, they could pack this evening and go in the morning, avoid Hugo, and while they were away, Arlene would speak to her brother on the phone and lay down the law, what he'd said to Cassie was a disgrace, he should be ashamed of himself, it was time for this passive aggressive (and now plain aggressive) bullying to stop, he was a father and had to take responsibility for the way he treated Cassie. Arlene promised she would beat the hell out of him — he deserved it.

`But I don't understand why he says those things ...` the eleven-year-old cried. `It's not my fault she died, it was cancer's fault, how can he say I had anything to do with it?`

`Because he's not right in the head. He never has been, and he never could hide it well. Don't pay any attention to him.`

`I can't help it if I babble. I really don't want to babble, it makes me sick.`

`Honey, try to relax, he's not here any more.`

'But he is, Auntie Arlene – he's right here all the time, in the house, I can't get away from him, I can't even lurk about in the shadows, even that's a provocation. He's got it the wrong way round, he can go anywhere he wants to but I'm only eleven, where can I go???'

'Tomorrow we'll go wherever you want.'

'But it's not forever, is it?'

Arlene looked at her sadly, as much for herself as her troubled, frightened niece.

A thought occurred to Cassie, which filled her with excitement. 'Andrew told me Mum left me money, can't I have it now, can't I leave this place, get a home of my own?'

'Darling, you're too young.'

'Anything to get away from him.'

Arlene hugged her. The little girl was weak in her grip. She tried to hug back but was too exhausted. 'Just relax,' she said.

'But it's not right, is it? I'm not responsible for Mum's death, am I?'

'Don't think that for a second. Just because your father's gone bananas, don't let him infect you too.'

It took a long time before she said: 'Okay ...'

Shattered, she fell into a bombardier sleep: nothing around her, the rest of the world thousands of feet below, passing by silently, little clouds of explosions in other peoples' lives, the peaceful drone of cruising at this altitude mesmeric. Arlene stayed by her side, stroking her hair, keeping an eye on the door lest Hugo's mania bring him back for more; or if Cassie woke startled, scared stiff by his words, she'd be there to correct misapprehensions that would otherwise bend her back and forth. Such protectiveness towards her niece, such sadness for this poor little girl. Laying there, wondering what it would be like if Cassie really was her daughter ...

Elsewhere in the house. In the confines of his bedroom. Hugo sat gazing at the lipstick book. Cassie's words ran over and over in his mind.

Another message from Lucy!

Cryptic of course: people don't recognise a message from the other side if it arrives without a mask; how disparaging he'd once been of matters irrational, yet the many disguises it took to bring him this message! Of course, had he not received the lipstick book, Cassie's comment would have remained a snippet of yet another verbal splurge. But he had, and what significance! For the lipstick novel, or to give it it's real and trashy name "The Forgotten of the Day Before", was about a scientific trip to the Bermuda Triangle, where modern-day equipment (from cameras to sensors to laser radar) would transmit every move of every person on that vessel, along with the ship itself, in an experiment into the long-standing mystery. A welcome break from semi-incomprehensible documents Hugo had to force his way through at work, he read it in a day and moved on to the next in his holiday library. A tale of sailors, their fate a mystery, when they entered the Triangle they too vanished, and all of their instruments fed back nothing to base camp, who had no idea what happened or where they'd gone. That's where the story ended, all of the sailors missing, their ship and instruments too, another victory struck for the Bermuda Triangle.

Though she'd babbled the sentence in one go, he'd picked up enough for the shudder to pass through him along with a thrill of delight. Slowed down from her lightning effusion, she had said:

A rumour that one of the sailors sent a message to their loved one by writing a code in a copy of a book that found its way to her almost four years later ...

For Cassie to start babbling on such a topic was too much of a coincidence, even for Andrew Faro: of the many theories of the disappearance of the Marie Celeste crew, one had been connected to the Bermuda Triangle. Nor had he told Cassie about the book, only the lawyer, who was obliged to confidentiality and wouldn't have breathed a word. Whatever Faro might think, Cassie had confirmed his certainty that there was a message in this book, and that it had been sent to him by his vanished soul mate. Lucy had said: ignore the naysayers! All he required now was time and resolve to break the code. He had all of the former he could possibly need and was happy to dedicate the rest of his life to this quest, if that's what it took.

Feverishly, he began to scan through "The Forgotten of the Day Before". He lingered for a while as he passed page 96. The outline of Lucy's lipstick, faded by the passing of more than a decade but so clearly her's, seemed to form words. He listened for their sound, for fragments of her, telling him a story, telling him off. What he heard sounded like it had been passed through an old-time record player, faded and diffused by archaic tech. He continued to read. Not a lengthy tome, 250-odd pages; traversed in a couple of hours, he skimmed the last page with no sense of a message contained between its covers. If it was in code, it would not be broken so easily.

Hugo lay on his bed – losing his temper left him shattered. An emptiness at having done so, the look on Cassie's face ... It involved extremities, an expulsion at a cellular level. Who knows when he'd have stopped raging had she not burbled that comment? Inside, he was fully aware: no time soon. The bed beneath him, some calm now: a rest after the tumult. Truth be told, Faro's unvarnished disdain had shaken his confidence, but now he felt so much better, and correct about the provenance of the lipstick novel. A plan of action was called for. He resolved to read "The Forgotten of the Day Before" three or four times every day until he broke the code. With that, he fell into a deep and dreamless sleep.

Cassie woke to find Arlene napping on the sofa in her room. The eleven-year-old had rested better than for many a recent night, thanks to her aunt, who'd braved discomfort and the wrath of Hugo to stay close by, to keep an eye on her, to be near if needed and protect her from further onslaught. Who knew what time the poor thing had dropped off? There was no need for her to be here, yet she was; Arlene had freedom and means, the two great pillars of modern life. She could be travelling around the world, going to all the right parties, having romances with squires and well-educated punks – enjoying herself the way people are supposed to want to. She could be far away from the comatose man and the mad little child, getting up late, staying up late, without worldly cares or pressure. Yet here she was, sleeping on the sofa in her room, crumpled and probably cold, just to be near her niece.

As if aware of the attention, Arlene's eyes began to open, stirring from her sleep. She saw Cassie looking back at her with a loving expression. Glad to see her niece was safe, she smiled. `What time is it?` she asked, yawning and stretching.

Cassie looked at her clock. `8.39. Did you sleep okay darling?`

`Absolutely fine. When did you wake up?`

`Just now.`

Arlene nodded. `Good.`

`Auntie ... Can we still go away?`

`Darling, of course.`

An hour later, they were showered, packed and ready to go. Arlene was alarmed to see Cassie trembling at the thought of entering the wider realm of the house, where Hugo was bound to roam at this time of day. Though after following her merciless pasting, this was no great surprise. Protective of her niece and hungering for vengeance, `I'll go first,` she said. `You stay close behind.`

Cassie nodded nervously.

Arlene opened the door to the pre-teen's bedroom. She walked outside. Cassie watched her go. Her heartbeat raced when she was alone. A few moments later, her aunt appeared again, to signal that the coast was clear. She picked up her travel bag and rapidly followed her outside.

Together, they walked along the short hall that led to the landing. Arlene motioned for Cassie to hang back. She then stepped brazenly out into open territory. Cassie held her breath, sighed relief when she saw from her aunt's expression that Hugo wasn't there. Arlene darted into the guest bedroom, and came out a few moments later with her overnight bag and coat. She motioned to Cassie, who took her cue to rush onto and across the landing, to a safe corner of wall where they both settled. Only Arlene could see down the extravagant staircase to the expanse of ground floor at its base.

`Is he there?` the eleven-year-old asked.

`I don't think so. I'm gonna go down.`

Arlene was about to descend the stairs when Cassie grabbed her arm. She looked at her niece, saw feral eyes, a terror that continued to expand.

`It'll be alright,` Arlene said, smiling. `You can trust me. Woman to woman.`

The little girl paused – then nodded. Arlene turned her gaze towards the bottom of the stairs. She stepped forward. Cassie didn't let go of her until she was too far away to hold on to. She watched her aunt descend with the dread fear of seeing someone you love move further into harm's way. With each step, Cassie could feel her chest tighten, the expectation that Hugo would leap out at Arlene, a velociraptor, and shred her to pieces. She thought she'd burst into tears fuelled by anxiety, but then her aunt was looking up at her from the danger zone and smiling, the coast clear. Cassie ran as fast as she could, hitting every third step before whizzing past Arlene, across the main hall, through the front door and out into her aunt's car, where she slammed the door shut, panting heavily, delighted at having escaped the maximum security prison.

Back inside the house, Arlene allowed her niece a little more time ... And then went to find her brother.

She saw Hugo through the back window, walking in the field. Deep in thought, probably wired on coffee, he looked like a lost horse in need of leading home. Much of her anger melted away. He was no better off than Cassie.

Calmer, she walked into the kitchen, grabbed some paper and a pen, wrote a short note saying that she and her niece were going away for a few days and would return by the weekend. Hugo was to call Arlene if necessary; if not, she'd be looking after Cassie, and he need know no more than that. She went into the dining room, left the note in the most visible part of the house: in his current vacant state, he needed all the help he could get.

They drove fast, talking all the way. Before Cassie knew it, they'd arrived again at the little guest house Arlene had taken her to last time. `We can go anywhere you want,` aunt had said when she'd got in the car after leaving the house. When niece conveyed her chosen destination, she responded, `Really?` Cassie nodded. `Well, that's fine by me, but we need to get you seeing more of the world before long.`

They had the same rooms as last time, with Cassie running into her's and leaping onto the bed and yelling in delight. Arlene shook her head, grinning: okay, that explains it: she wants some familiarity in her troubled little life. Arlene settled into her own room, and they were just in time for a long, late, sumptuous lunch at the town's best restaurant, where their conversation continued unabated, ranging across many subjects and a variety of emotions, allowing the strain to lift from Cassie's face (and Arlene's too), vanishing in the long shadows of the late afternoon and the evening's balmy nonchalance.

More than a hundred miles away, Hugo had seen Arlene's note. It made no impact on him. All he could think of was the unbroken code in the lipstick novel. In the space of a day, he'd re-read the book but discovered nothing more, and learnt nothing else that may bring him closer to cracking its meaning.

He fired up his brain with repeated shots of coffee, wondering if he shouldn't move his chair into the kitchen to be within arm's reach of the machine. His intelligence had long-since skewed towards the demands of work, but in his younger days he'd enjoyed a powerful imagination. He was calling on it now for the first time in twenty years. But it seemed to have grown rusty from lack of use: it failed to function, flickering and punting and hissing and growling but never catching hold of whatever was staring him in the face. He ran his mind up alleyways with nothing at the end but dismissal; he started to shake from coffee O.D., and yet still drank more, filling his cup, his body with caffeine. His brain augured weak signals from the book, nowhere near enough to decipher the code.

Later in the day, Cassie realised Hugo hadn't called to make sure she was okay. A wave of sadness washed over her, for though she may not want to see him, she longed to think he was missing her just the tiniest bit. Arlene had been sworn to a grave promise that she'd tell Cassie if he called; her niece made the same vow. Neither had cause to declare. Hugo was probably loving his time alone, the eleven-year-old thought. Maybe he's hoping I'll never came back.

Not that she wasn't having some much needed fun herself. Arlene and she moved from the restaurant to a riverside coffee house. The owner knew Arlene and was delighted to make the acquaintance of her niece. They settled at a table watching the quiet water roll past, its flecks and contours picked out by the moon. The run of their conversation had remained unbroken since they'd set off; Cassie still had acres of unused nervous energy. Arlene was ever-more enchanted by her troubled travelling companion, whose dazzling personality expanded the longer they were away from Hugo. Eventually – regrettably – it was the adult who had to go to bed, lest she conk out across the coffee house table. They had a chatty five minute walk back to their guest house, and kissed each other goodnight with Arlene's promise that, despite her exhaustion, if Cassie needed her for anything, anything at all, she'd be there in a second.

On her own in her room, the eleven-year-old cleaned up, changed and got into bed. As she settled beneath the sheets, she realised how tired she was – for the first time in a while, pleasantly so. She closed her eyes and agreed with herself that she really did like Arlene, and that if she wanted to be a stronger presence in her life, then that was fine by Cassie. She was so entertaining, so different from her father; perhaps they'd grown up on different planets! When they spoke, it was as if Arlene really did think of Cassie as a grown up: inexperienced and not very big but with an intelligence that demanded respect, and engagement on an equal plane. Their conversation ranged across subjects that even Lucy hadn't introduced her to, like politics, philosophy, art and history. So many stories! And she was such a great teller of these tales, it made Cassie want to listen to more of them, more of her, the woman, so keen to lavish all this pent-up attention and affection when in the past she'd been somewhat far-flung.

Wearied by this thinking, Cassie let go of the consciousness with which she'd been struggling and began to descend to sleep, ah, bliss!

What relief there could be in the freedom of nocturnal fantasy! Far away from her father, and remembering now whilst deep asleep to keep the doors, the windows, the whole house open in case her mother chose to contact her through the midnight medium as well as the living day, she was starting to dream more, but it was Arlene who was often in them, not Lucy. They would walk together, on dazzling journeys across mountains riding elephants and through canyons soaring aloft on birds, meeting exotic creatures and even more exotic people, and there'd be no tension, no fear. Every man they met would look nothing like Hugo, every house they visited would have rainbows for side lamps and soft coral for duvets. There was school but only if she wanted it, there were parties without end, but early nights too; and so she waited – full of hope! – to hear from her mother again soon, in this realm or the waking.

The triple tone of her mobile phone announced the arrival of a text. She sat up immediately, grabbed the sparkling handset. Saw the words and name.

"your father needs you" the text said. And the sender's name: "Mum".

8

It was late in the night before the morning came. Hugo was sick with caffeine engorgement and still in yesterday's clothes. He'd read the lipstick book more than a dozen times, starting again at the beginning the moment his eyes passed over the last word. So far it had told him nothing, and now he was starting to worry that the more he read it, the further beneath its surface the code would sink. But if he didn't persevere, how would he find out what Lucy was trying to tell him? He felt utterly stupid, lacking talent for anything, not just the breaking of a code. How easy it was for his sense of self to be smashed to pieces with Lucy no longer around to keep him on track. She was trying to help him from afar but he needed her here! Utterly frustrated, wired by his body's caffeine aggregation, home alone with no one to see, the big question fell upon him.

He knew what Cassie and Arlene thought of him, could see it in their faces, their disbelief at his inability to communicate. No one sympathised that he'd lost his wife. His daughter could argue the same, while his sister knew him too well to feel compassionate towards him – at least that would be her excuse. Frustrated by their expectation that he should grieve in such a way as to satisfy them, regardless of how he actually felt, or of how he was built to lament, perhaps he was no more than a gibbering fool bent completely out of shape by tragedy, spouting colossal tripe, with signs of diminished responsibility. Disdain was worse than pity; it didn't mean they were wrong.

And here, alone in the house, his wife dead, his child taken to safer climes by his sister, even ridiculed by his attorney, Hugo wondered if it was worth carrying on. Had Arlene divined the onset of this epiphany, and realised she needed to get Cassie away from him so her father could set his mind permanently to rest? With no one around to stop him, no one would know for days – no chance of unwanted interruptions. A variety of methods to choose from, as befit a society that prided itself on the choices it gave the consumer: the bathroom with sleeping pills by the truckload for those living in a house of the dying; a streamline commercial burglar-repelling pistol in a locked cabinet beside his bed; an expensive barber shop razor set bought for him by a grateful client (viz. the law of unintended consequences); two cars in the garage that could pump out carbon monoxide to a high level of performance ... No end of ways to end his days.

Hugo settled on the "monoxide poisoning while sitting in his favourite car" option. The other methods were too gruesome, and in all likelihood, Cassie and Arlene would find him. A sprawl of slasher mess would introduce an element of shock he knew wouldn't be there if he killed himself in a less visually abrupt way. That they'd find him asleep in his car would ease them into the eventuality, rather than throwing over them a bucket of poison they'd never be able to clean away. (He cast from his mind the thought that they might actually prefer to see him mangled beyond recognition.)

He needed hose pipe. Connect it to the car's exhaust, feed the other end through a window open just enough to let the pipe in but not so wide as to allow the fumes to escape before they'd done their job. Set the engine running, suck in the dust, sit back and float away. A hut on the edge of the field behind the house contained their gardening tools. Hugo trudged towards it. Cool air danced across his tight skin. Barefoot, the apathetic grass ignored his feet. The taste of coffee dried in his mouth.

He turned around, spinning on a square inch, went running back into the house, a frenzied gait, leaping up the stairs three at a time, rushing along the landing, almost broke the door off its hinges as he flew into his bedroom, reached out in a photo finish stretch and with greed for an item that belonged to him picked up "The Forgotten of the Day Before", rocketed to page 96 and hungrily read the paragraph across which Lucy had laid her smooch more than a decade ago, a paragraph which said "And Captain Henderson brought his face close to the screen. `Your call, my friend,` he said to his partner. `But I would like to see my daughter again.`

Valetta considered the data, and saw his opportunity. `My needs are simple,` he replied. `It's time you and I came to a financial arrangement.`"

Hugo's eyes darted through the paragraph. Almost blurring with the strain, he forced himself to focus on the words upon which the lipstick itself had fallen, words that were blindingly obvious now he knew what to see. Blinking at this juncture of anxiety and excitement, the words within the paragraph highlighted by the lipstick began to emerge from the paragraph itself, lining up one-by-one to create a new short sentence previously hidden which, when pieced together, presented before his tearful expression – tears of joy! – the long-sought and much hallowed message from Lucy!

Your.

Daughter.

Needs.

You.

He almost flinched at the impact, though he'd been struck by no one, nor a stranger take a swipe at him and miss. His blood still racing through a sense of hope, of lust ... And now its gentle fading, into ... a state of complete confusion. Hugo lay on the bed. Thought about the sentence. Stared at the ceiling. Thought about the sentence. Looked at the words upon which the lipstick had fallen. Thought about the sentence. Read it through once more.

Your daughter needs you.

Thought about the sentence …

Cassie was equally thrown, not just by the arrival of the second text from "Mum", but by the message it contained. She couldn't sleep after its appearance, a long night, a storm of confusion, for just as she thought she was coming to terms with Hugo – in that the less time she spent with him the better – the one person she'd longed to hear from was telling her to run back to him, to look after him, to sustain him. In the joy of the sense that her mother was out there somewhere, she had to change direction: do not consider your own feelings, Lucy was saying: your father needs you.

And yet there it was, the second text. She had to focus on this momentous development, for the line was open, the opportunity to speak with her mother real. Cassie experienced pain and pleasure at the same time. There were so many things she wanted to say to Lucy, so many questions she wanted to ask. She gripped her mobile phone and typed out a long message of love to her deceased but conscious mother, full of delight and need. She was about to send it when she paused for a moment, and thought about the second text. Why that message? she asked herself. Cassie didn't know, and suddenly felt a peculiar yet powerful need to hold off before sending another. She deleted the one she was poised to dispatch before it could make its way into the cosmic ether; this very clever girl was condemned to another bout of very deep thought.

Arlene noticed something amiss as soon as she collected her niece on their way to breakfast. Exhausted again after such a good job of unwinding yesterday, had the eleven-year-old not slept at all? If so, what had kept her awake? Immediately, she asked: `Darling, are you alright?`

Cassie looked at her, and where in the past she might have nodded to cover her tracks (however unconvincingly), she felt immense relief that her aunt was here, and asking this very question. Without saying any more, she thrust out her phone.

Arlene's brow furrowed as she took the handset. She went pale as she read the text. She looked at Cassie, who took the phone back, brought up the first text from Lucy, and showed her that too. Arlene blanched. Cassie watched her, eyes wide and focused, waiting for guidance, needing her to help.

`Let's go eat,` was all Arlene said.

She and Cassie sat at their table. Breakfast continued around them. Her aunt hardly touched her coffee. Cassie slowly munched through a big bowl of cereal without tasting anything. Both texts – and the invisible presence of Lucy – weighed heavily upon them. Cassie felt the drag of her sleepless night, wondered if she'd ever rest again. Arlene was suddenly powerless, lacking any influence, trumped.

It was almost clearing up time in the restaurant when she said, `Have you told Hugo about this? I mean, the first one?`

The eleven-year-old shook her head vigorously.

`Have you told anyone? Andrew Faro maybe?`

Again, Cassie nodded in the negative.

Arlene sighed. They sat in silence.

`I think it's time I had more coffee,` she said eventually. Looking at her punchy, pale niece, `I think it's time you had some too ...`

They had to vacate the restaurant; there were many places for them to dissolve to while they considered what the hell was going on. But telling her aunt about the texts had the effect of freeing Cassie to sleep. After breakfast, she was getting ready to head out when, overcome with exhaustion, she lay down on her bed and dropped off. When Cassie didn't appear a few minutes later, her aunt gave her a little longer ... a little longer ... a little longer ... and then flew into a blind panic that something terrible had happened. She went running to the reception to ask her owner friend to let her in to Cassie's room. When they both put their heads around the door and found the eleven-year-old snoring away, Arlene's pulse slowed by an extensive percentage. She let Cassie sleep, and went back to her room to wait for her to wake.

Her mind was a blank and pained by this development. Her niece had explained how she'd checked with Andrew whether or not Lucy's phone would still have been connected at the time the first text was sent, or within the possession of anyone who knew them. He'd confirmed that it would not have been. So in trying to determine where they came from, the existence of the first text could be excused as a mere random happenstance, a crosswire. But even ignoring the improbability of receiving two texts by mistake, the second was far too specific to Cassie to be anything other than deliberate. And far too onerous. The pre-teen had gazed at her, longing for Arlene to endorse her most deeply held hope: that Lucy was getting in touch.

But it couldn't be from Lucy. Arlene held herself back from saying these destructive words. She wanted to scream them out, bring sense to this insensible situation. The notion that Cassie's dead mother was contacting her from beyond the grave – and of all means, by text – and telling her to look after her father was so obviously insane it was even more corrosive than Hugo's terminal mood. Wanting it to be true didn't make it so.

And yet ... What about that second text?

Arlene had had ex-boyfriends (and an ex-husband) who hanged around with the same odious unavoidability of that second text. Whichever way she turned, there it was, blocking her off, demanding answers she didn't have, spoiling her notions of how things could be, if only Cassie would just ... But as with all those ex-whatevers, the texts had to be dealt with, for she couldn't pretend her niece hadn't received them – and nor did Cassie want to, which was the real problem.

As if the presence of the second text wasn't trouble enough, its content was flat out bizarre. Of all the messages a dead mother may have for her young daughter, why this one??? Surely Lucy should have imparted a little more wisdom: an order that Cassie look after a man who rejected all of her attempts to do so, rejected her entirely? This cruel treatment, from wherever it came, was not only mal-intended but misunderstood what was now happening in the lives of the father and daughter.

`It's definitely not from Lucy,` Arlene said to herself, as she paced around her room. She wouldn't have been so cruel.

The sunny morning was sliding into an overcast afternoon. She'd wait until Cassie woke of her own accord, they didn't need to be anywhere else. She opened her window and glared at the world at peace, jealous of its composure.

Her mobile phone began to ring. She walked over to it, looked at the caller.

Took a veeeeeeery deep breath and then pressed the button to accept the call. She began, `If you're going to yell at me for giving Cassie a break then ...`

Hugo said, `Something strange has happened.`

She almost laughed, yeah - tell me about it.

`Lucy has contacted me,` he said.

Arlene felt herself go still. Oh Lord, she thought: they're both cracking up on me.

`Arlene?`

`Well ... What do you want me to say?`

He started telling her about the lipstick book, about the promise Lucy and he had made each other years ago, about how he'd found the book in his local second hand store – Lucy knew how much he loved that place – how he was certain beyond a shadow of a doubt it was the same book she'd kissed in Australia more than a decade ago, how Lucy had sent it to him to keep her promise, that it contained a coded message, and having only just deciphered the code, it wasn't the message he'd been expecting. His daughter needed him, Lucy had told him – and now he didn't know what to do.

Halfway through this uncharacteristically verbose outpour, Arlene thought of telling him about the texts Cassie had received. Likewise, if she should tell her niece about Hugo's revelation. Separately, they sounded as barmy as the other, but when combined, the dangers arising from this toxic brew were as numerous as they were ugly. Neither Hugo nor Cassie would be able to move on if they thought Lucy was trying to contact them, that they could communicate with her, and if they both believed it was true – having been so inspired by separate sources, bolstering their certainty that the messages were not mis-directed one-offs or coincidence – they'd reinforce each other's delusions, adding another dose of years to the fantasy, inundating themselves for so long they'd never live their lives again. They had to mourn, grieve, do what it took for as long as necessary, but first they had to accept that Lucy was dead. Yet it may already be too late. As well as the two texts supposedly from her mother, Cassie had shown Arlene the text she'd sent in response to the first, where daughter addressed mother directly, as if she were truly alive, as if she would respond again. Which she had appeared now to have done.

Hugo had stopped talking. He was waiting for Arlene to speak. She was flustered by her thoughts, her deductions about where this may go. She had little patience for him at the best of times; she kicked back reflexively.

`What do I think?` she said, answering the rhetorical question, the one he'd asked by his pause. `What do I think? I think you sound like you jumped off a mountain and landed on your head. You think Lucy is trying to contact you from beyond the grave??? Did you listen to yourself when you said that??? It's insane; it's worse – it's morbid, borderline psycho-necrophiliac. What about Cassie??? You're not the only person caught up in this; a little girl is longing for the tiniest show of affection from her father. I'm trying to help her relax, we're gonna be here for another three days, like I said in my note. What do I think??? I think you need to get your head together, and stop talking like you had a lobotomy.`

`But Arlene ...`

`BUT ARLENE WHAT?!!!` she screamed. `ARLENE, PLEASE??? IS THAT WHAT YOU WERE GOING TO SAY??? THAT SUDDENLY I'D BELIEVE LUCY WAS CONSCIOUS SOMEWHERE IN THE COSMOS AND MAKING YOU A PART OF HER INTERSTELLAR BOOK CLUB??? NO, HUGO, NO! YOU HAVE A DAUGHTER, YOU NO LONGER HAVE A WIFE. YOU HAVE TO GET THIS INTO YOUR IGNORANT, MORONIC MIND, OR ELSE YOU'LL LOSE CASSIE JUST LIKE YOU LOST LUCY, AND THIS TIME YOU WON'T HAVE ANYONE TO BLAME BUT YOURSELF.`

She hung up on him. Sat there, in her room, the pressure crushing down upon her, angry and alarmed by this turns of events, wondering how to advise her niece who'd soon wake up in need of answers, the only kind being those she wouldn't want to hear and which may drive her away just when they were getting close.

She wondered what Hugo's expression now was, following that volley. Had she been standing in front of him, she'd have seen a terrified look in his eyes, him rooted to the ground, yet floating in space, scared he'd never settle again. She'd feel guilty and relieved, for she didn't want to shatter his hopes but couldn't permit him to quench his agony by indulging in such fancy. And what did he want, a medal for working out that Cassie needed him??? That he had to be told this by a book besmirched with lipstick??? Guilty because she enjoyed hitting him hard, because he deserved it for how he'd treated his daughter, how he'd treated her. Guilty that he might already have flipped, that it was too late to prevent the damage from being permanent. Guilty that she had no sympathy for him. Relieved that if his comatose state and outbursts were driven by this ridiculous notion then the sooner it was brought to an end, the better.

There was a knock; it broke the daze she'd fallen into. She unlocked her door to see the beautiful, open face of Cassie.

`You're supposed to be resting!` Arlene said, starting to cry as she bundled her niece into a wholesale loving hug, which seemed to cuddle every cell in Cassie's body. The eleven-year-old was surprised by the intensity of her emotion but was soon hugging her back.

`Honey, did you manage to get some sleep?` aunt said when they sat down on the bed, and she was straightening out her niece's hair.

Cassie didn't answer. Instead, she handed Arlene her phone. She took it, eyebrows crumpling on her forehead, saw the message her niece had sent. "But he doesn't love me" it said. The recipient: "Mum".

Arlene looked at Cassie, and noticed her sad, hopeful expression. She felt her heart sink. `Oh, my ... Well, why don't we see what happens now ...`

9

Arlene called Hugo to let him know they were coming back. He didn't answer. She left a voicemail with the exact time of their return, and informed him that she hadn't told Cassie of his purported message from Lucy. An incendiary act at this tricky time, but someone had to maintain a semblance of sanity in this disintegrating family.

Cassie had two reasons to grow downcast. First, as the days of their trip counted down to their return, she received no response to her latest text to Lucy. Filled with excitement after she'd sent it, once a day had passed with no rejoinder she grew anxious: if Lucy was so keen to correspond, why was she so slow in replying? Would she text again? Second, in direct proportion to her anxiety over the lack of a response from her mother, the prospect of being sited within the same airspace as her father left her feeling many varieties of ill. The drive home assumed the tone of a return to an execution: the trial occurred, the conviction made, the sentence imposed and now to be carried out. As chatty as they'd been on the outbound journey, so long doleful silences undermined their previous breezy calm. The unknown knowns, the known unknowns, and worst of all: the known knowns. And then the sight of the house itself, inevitable; to run for the best part of a week only to find themselves back where they started. The inner contamination rendered its exterior faded and cold. Arlene switched off the engine. They sat there, mute.

`I don't want to go in,` the eleven-year-old said.

`I don't want to go in either,` the aunt replied.

The tension surrounding their return received an additional boost from a third concern, perhaps the greatest of all. Shortly before they'd set off on their journey home, the eleven-year-old had raised the prospect of going to live with Arlene.

`Of course!!!` she'd exclaimed, the moment the request came out of Cassie's mouth. `I have so much room you can take as much as you like! We can stay up late talking to each other, we can have parties, you can bring your friends, we can go travelling, and when you get interested in boys I'll interrogate them to make sure they're suitable but in such a charming way they won't even know! And then when you're a bit older we'll ...` The immense and obvious delight was suddenly tempered by the reality of their situation. `Oh, but ... it's not my decision. Though it's like being cared for by a zombie, your father's still your legal guardian. He may have flipped, but the authorities would still say he's the one in charge. So ... if it's fine by him, it's absolutely fine by me.`

The time had come to put the question to him. Cassie was on tenterhooks about how he may react. Dealing with these adults was such a strange and scary business – at times like this she didn't feel like a woman at all, nor even a hardy eleven-year-old. The prospect of raising the issue in the first place, let alone announcing her preferred option, rumbled with heavy boots over lazy buttercups: she could easily see the enmeshed mess her request / demand would provoke. How much happier it had been to ask Arlene if she could live with her: aunt responded with the right amount of unalloyed delight. But Hugo hated her so much that although he'd be overjoyed to offload this walking irritant he may deny her just to deny her. Arlene sat next to her in the car, but she might as well have been on the other side of the universe. The house foreboding, no echoes from within. A mausoleum indeed. The still of the vehicle, after hours of rumbling and vibrating and whirring and whispering, lurching deeply into the moment.

`Do you want me to go and talk to him first?` Arlene asked.

After a long pause, her niece replied, `No.`

Aunt looked at her brave little soldier. `Tell you what. I'll wait here for 15 minutes. Then I'll come in. How about that?`

`Deal,` Cassie said, almost biting her hand off.

They hugged awkwardly across the gear stick and handbrake. Arlene kissed her niece on the forehead. Cassie took a deep breath and stepped out of the car. She walked to the front door, ten times bigger than she. Wrangling her keys, agitated, fingers and thumbs, finally she managed to unlock the front door and go inside.

`Good luck,` Arlene whispered.

The front door closed behind Cassie. She had slammed her eyes shut. As she stood in the hall near the base of the extravagant staircase, she heard nothing. Slowly, she lifted her eyelids to gaze upon the wide open plain of the house, which now felt utterly dead having been bereft of she and Arlene these last few days. Hugo was nowhere to be seen. She couldn't even sense he was here. She started to walk through, wondering where her father may be. Her heart was racing. As soon as she saw him, she'd ask to be liberated from this grand manse of doom. She mouthed silently the words she'd use, ready to deliver them as soon as he appeared. She scanned every corner and crevice as if she were in unknown territory behind enemy lines.

No sign of him in the kitchen, nor the dining room. He wasn't even in his staring chair, looking across the field, into infinity. Nowhere to be found on the ground floor, Cassie ascended the staircase and continued a higher altitude hunt for him. His bedroom door was wide open. She looked inside. The room was empty, the bed made. Strange. She walked through to the en-suite bathroom. He wasn't there either. She went back out onto the landing and checked the guest bedrooms, including the one that provided temporary home to Arlene. Still no Hugo.

She even checked her own bedroom, though she knew he wouldn't be there: he always respected her private space. She dropped off her bag, shook off her coat, wondered where else to look.

`DAD?` she called out. Her voice echoed through the landing, down the stairs and into the ground floor hall. But he didn't answer.

Cassie descended the staircase, walked through the hall into the lounge, passed her father's empty chair and looked out of the window that gazed upon the field. She scanned the horizon, from the far right to the far left, where the garage lay. At last a sign of life: she could hear an engine running.

She walked out the side door and crossed the paved area between the house and garage where in happier times Lucy had made marvellous barbeques. Without her coat she was cold, nestling into her jumper. The sound of the engine running from inside the garage grew louder the closer she got. Her first thought was that Hugo may be about to drive off – but he hadn't driven anywhere yet, and she'd heard the engine for at least a minute now, and it might have been chugging for a while before she noticed it.

A spasm of concern – something's wrong.

Cassie started to run. She reached for the garage side door. Couldn't open it. Locked from the inside.

`DAD!` she yelled, banging on the portal. She ran to the garage's front doors. They too were closed.

She rattled the panels. `LET ME IN!` But they didn't give. Nor were they opened from the inside.

Cassie stood still, panicking. It was no great secret her father was depressed but it hadn't occurred to her that he might do something silly. He was inside the garage, inside a car, the engine running and now all she could think about was the times she hadn't gone to sit with him when he'd been in the depths of grief, when she'd avoided him to avoid his difficult character – but maybe he'd just been sad and needed her, just like her mother had said in the text. A rapid upsurge of despairing remorse took hold of her, a sense of a disloyalty committed against him, he whose inability to cope had only now became apparent – just when it was too late, when he was in the locked garage trying to kill himself – perhaps had already done so.

Get Arlene, she said to herself. *Get Arlene.*

But she'd heard Arlene scream a heavy volley at Hugo on the first night of their trip, although the walls of her bedroom had muffled her words so Cassie hadn't been able to hear what she was shouting about. Of course, Cassie knew she was the most likely topic, but what if other stuff had come out too, older stuff, stuff from the past? From the tone of some of her anecdotes, it didn't take a genius to recognise that Hugo and Arlene had had a difficult relationship over the years – she so effervescent, he so dead to the world – and now she had a reason – a person – to justify attack after attack if she were so minded. But in doing so, in unloading upon him a blitzkrieg, had Arlene contributed to this suicide attempt? Would she welcome it??? The final barrier to custody of Cassie removed, the life she had been campaigning for, hers? If so, could she – would she – help???

She was stricken by these thoughts, unable to move. The scale of this adult business overwhelmed her. And what if it was too late any way??? He might already be dead. He might have sucked his last monoxide breath feeling he was glad to be free of it all, including she; he might have been terrified when at last he went under. Oh Lord, she thought, I'm an orphan, what am I going to do, how am I going to live without either of my parents??? The senseless normality of this familiar scenery, the path between the house and the garage she knew so well, a scene of dread: her father dead. I'm an orphan, I don't want to be an orphan, I want my dad, I want ...

The side door opened. There stood Hugo. Cassie spluttered with relief. She wanted to rush towards him, but her delight was tempered by her fear.

`What are you doing???` she yelped.

He stared at her, subsumed by the intensity of her gaze, by the fear of his death it spoke of, by a fear he was sure wasn't there, by a love for him he was convinced she didn't have, by the absence of his certainty that she didn't care if he lived or died. Her breathing was rapid, her skin paler than his, her eyes open as far as they could go. He'd scared her. She was calming from the extremes the body reaches when in the grip of the panic – brace yourself – but the imprint of terror was in the air around her. It filtered into the space between them, mixing with his outline, the perimeter of the ocean, the remote territory the man had become.

`I was ... running the engine ... because it's been ... sitting there for ... weeks ... and ... needed ... turning over ...`

She stared at him, unsure whether to buy it. Again she felt far too young for this – a child, not a woman at all – and never should have been called one. But as her body continued to relax, so too did her expression. She'd seen nothing to prove her father wrong, so he might have been telling the truth. But her alarm curdled into anger that he may have been trying to kill himself, that he would rob her of her only living parent. Her face grew hard, but feeding into this dismay was a sense of shock, slightly delayed. Now she felt older, now she felt old. She shook her head, an implicit rebuke. He was shaken by a face so much more certain than when he'd seen her last, all of four days ago. At the back of their minds and on their tips of their tongues: their orders from Lucy. And yet face-to-face, even now the sheer breach of secrecy involved in divulging these messages kept them silent.

Hugo and Cassie looked towards the house.

'You need to talk,` said Arlene. 'Why don't the both of you come inside?`

And so father sat with daughter, and daughter sat with father, as if they were strangers. The dining room table vast, the distance between them immeasurable. Arlene was present, an unwilling umpire, sure she should be anywhere but here. Hugo was pale, dark circles around bloodshot eyes. He coughed, needed a shower, looked as if he had something to hide. Cassie's mouth was open, her eyes fixed on him. If she wanted to say what she came here to say, she'd have to form the words sooner or later. But something had happened in these few minutes, and they were now in No-Man's Land.

This impasse persisted for minutes before Arlene said, 'How about a drink? Cassie, honey, will you give me a hand?`

In the kitchen, she said to her niece, 'I'm not helping. The two of you have to speak without me getting in the way. I'm going to go upstairs, have a shower, read, watch T.V., whatever. If at any point you need me, I'm ten seconds away, darling. Okay? Never forget that: I'm here, anytime you need me.`

The eleven-year-old wanted nothing less than for her aunt to leave. And Arlene wanted very much to stay. 'But these are the things,` she said, nodding, hoping that that would be explanation enough.

Cassie understood, but didn't really; nor did Arlene, who grasped it perfectly well.

Drinks made, leave taken, the table seemed larger, more troubling, now it was just the two of them, father and daughter sans interpolator. Another espresso for Hugo, a juice for Cassie, and the silence that followed the sound of the engine stopped, and the endlessness of their days of mourning.

`Dad ...` she began. `I ... I ...` The words were close but he so far away. Her mind's ear still fed her the sound of the car's engine. Yet knowing he was too brittle, too lost in mourning to be capable of looking after her, before she could consider their import, `I want to go and live with Arlene,` she said, hearing her request at the same time as Hugo, the words echoing across the table and back and forth against the dining room walls.

He didn't react. He hardly seemed to move. He stared into the espresso cup, the black pool of coffee ready to engulf him.

`Did you hear what I said?`

He looked up at her – yes, he had. His eyes were red, blistering but dry. No tears. He might have been sitting in the car trying to kill himself, caught in the act by his only child who tells him that she wants to move out though she's only a pre-teen, and still he is unable to cry! How Lucy had loved having a daughter, they could cry and cry together! Not like these broken boys who seemed only to sob at the wrong moment, if ever.

Hugo said, `Your home ... is here.`

`No ...` she replied. `My home ... was with Mum.`

`And with me.`

She shook her head.

`Cassie ...?`

`I want ... to be somewhere ... I'm ... not ... afraid.`

He was still, for a long time. And then he looked at her, his eyes a little redder, a little more sunk in his skull. `Cassie ... I don't ... want you ... to go.`

She churned inside. The eleven-year-old fixed her 42-year-old father with as tough a glare as she could manage, and said, `Well, it's not ... it's not ... You know, it's not ... It's just not up for discussion.`

As the words came out, they dissolved in her mouth. She wanted to be strong and meant what she said; she wasn't so sure she wanted to be strong, and didn't really know if she meant what she said.

It was his turn to speak, but he wasn't speaking.

`I can't help it when I babble,` she said, filling the vacuum. `It makes me feel so bad, and Arlene doesn't mind ... And she loves me. And ... I need to be loved.` Her voice catching, she stopped.

It was ridiculous that they should live here any way. Better to be free of the burden of the memory of good times unrecoverable. A happier regime could emerge again elsewhere, from walls, plaster, a lounge and kitchen that didn't always scream out Lucy. A life available at Arlene's. Cassie knew she wouldn't be able to say any more. All she had to do was leave. Just summon up the courage to stand, walk, ascend the staircase, go to Arlene's room, formally announce, and they could go ... The sooner she did that, the sooner she'd be ...

`Long ago,` Hugo said, his voice breaking through the petrified hush. `Before you were born ... Your mother and I ... made a promise to one another that ... if ... either of us ... died, we'd contact the one ... who was still alive. To let them know that we were close by ... watching over them.`

Now his eyes seemed a little less red, a little more emergent from their sunken pools of monoxide grief.

`Well ...` he said. `She's kept her promise.`

Cassie practically exploded inside.

`Do you believe me?` he asked.

She looked at him, unblinking.

He felt his coffee-cloaked mouth go dry. His massive news, the news he'd expected to floor her – to put a gigantic smile on her face – left him facing the same expression reserved for the village idiot. And then ... Slowly ...

She nodded.

By the simple vertical movement of her head, by acknowledging that he was not going insane, five years of grief vanished from his face. And there, for the first time since Lucy's cancer diagnosis, was a glimmer of the man she knew her father could be:

serious, quiet but tender in his own reserved way. She hadn't realised how much of a delight it would be to see him again, replacing even if only for a few moments the automaton who looked like her father and sounded like him on the very rare occasions he spoke but who beyond that was a stranger: the father who must have loved her – once upon a time.

Quietly she said, `She's contacted me too.`

Her comment drew his unutterable surprise. Refreshed by ten years now!!! The happiest kind of disbelief at this most miraculous of moments. And then it struck them at the same time: how obvious!

Of course she'd reach out to them both.

10

Andrew Faro was not surprised when the third member of the family settled into the chair on the other side of his desk, to partake of his advice. He'd not that long since spoken with Arlene about her divorce; he was certain this visit was on account of Hugo, their meeting informal to the point of invisible. In truth, Faro had been worrying about the sane and cautious man he knew for fifteen years ever since he came to say his dead wife had sent him a coded message in a book that took more than a decade to travel half way around the world. Had he told his sister? Was Arlene wondering if, short of sectioning the man, a plan of action was required; at least a discussion as to what she should do???

`Thanks for seeing me,` she said.

`No problem at all,` Faro replied. `What's up?`

`This is off the record, nothing legal.`

`Sure.`

`My brother you know well, Cassie too.`

`What an enchanting young lady she is.`

Arlene nodded. `She really is something special. I adore her. Since Lucy died, we've become ... close. She has bags of talent, she's such a sweetheart.`

`You're a very talented family.`

`A nuts family more like ...`

`But you didn't come to rave about your niece ...`

'No,' she said, oppressed, depressive. 'This is delicate and ... because it will sound insane. And I know it is insane, but the thing is, I'm not sure that I know what ... I should do. I know what I want to do. But I'm here to see if you need to talk me out of it, to make sure there's nothing I've missed.'

Faro listened as Arlene explained that father and daughter believed Lucy had contacted them.

The lawyer thought, both?

'Sounds crazy, I know,' she said. 'I'm scared that it is. Hugo thinks Lucy has sent him a message in a book. And Cassie has received two text messages from ... someone whose number appears in her phone book as "Mum".'

The lawyer remembered the call he'd received from the eleven-year-old asking him about the cancellation of her mother's mobile phone contract. An odd request at the time, but an odd time for the girl. Now he realised it wasn't just a random piece of nuttiness. He was all the more impressed by this remarkably self-possessed young woman.

'Cassie has sent a text to the number,' Arlene explained. 'She's told Hugo all about it and now they're both waiting on tenterhooks for a reply!'

'Good Lord ...'

'They believe Lucy's still alive or, well, if not alive then out there, somewhere, watching over them, watching from on high, keeping them safe, and if she's not gone then they don't have to mourn her, or come to terms with life without her. And if I say anything it makes me look wicked, evil – like I'm the one insisting they've both got it wrong, that it couldn't possibly be that way. And they'll think I'm … pushing in. Trying to take what's not mine. And it's two against one! They want to believe it so badly nothing else matters to Hugo, while as for Cassie ...`

Arlene paused. A look of deep sadness in her eyes, staring down at the desk as if she were thinking of good times lost – or good times very nearly had.

She raised her gaze, saw Faro gazing at her sadly.

The lawyer said, `I had no idea it was this bad.`

She nodded. `They're sitting around the house ...` she replied, annoyed by the existence of her own frustrated hopes. `I feel like there's nothing I can ...`

`What are they doing?`

`Just waiting.`

`For what?`

`A text from Lucy.`

Faro frowned. `But you say that … that Cassie received two text messages?`

She nodded, and told him of their content.

His brow uncurled slightly. `But perhaps the good news is that they're behaving better towards each other?` the lawyer asked. `Having been "told" by Lucy that they should look after one another?`

Arlene shook her head. `No, that's not the case. Despite the outbreak of peace, they're still like strangers. Strangers who know each other.`

A self-serving analysis, but Arlene may be right. In the cold house, beneath a sense of uneasy rapprochement, neither father nor daughter felt comfortable with each other. Hugo stood at the coffee machine, preparing an espresso. Cassie sat in the lounge, sitting on the sofa, reading. Her mobile phone was close to hand. The long-awaited triple-tone hadn't yet sounded a third time. Nonetheless, Hugo would react to the tune, whichever played for whichever friend texted her. He'd look at Cassie. She'd shake her head. He'd decline back into his coffee reverie. If he left the room, or if Cassie went elsewhere, or in the morning, he'd ask the inevitable question. And again, each time, she'd say no, there was as yet no third text from Lucy.

In the strange bond of their common pursuit, a semblance of routine settled into the household. Hugo began to treat his coffee-making as a craft, using the same dedication by which a watchmaker would render his latest bespoke time piece. He started to entertain thoughts of becoming a professional barista. Shortly before she died, Lucy gave Cassie a flute, an instrument she played in her youth and by which she hoped in parting legacy to encourage her child to be musical. The pre-teen was unsure if an instrumentalist lurked within, but one had to pass the time somehow. She felt talentless, yet no one need know she'd tried, apart from Hugo, who barely opened his mouth anyway. She passed her father as he made his precision ~~coffee on her way~~ to her bedroom. They may exchange no words, but the understanding was implicit: I will tell you if she responds. With that, she'd spend the next few hours grappling with the vagaries of the flautist's trade.

While hearing the music coming falteringly from his child's room, Hugo would compose texts to Lucy, long love notes, in which he'd say so much, what he hadn't said to her while she was alive, even when she was dying, things he hoped she knew but after her death realised she may not have. The coffee helped him to compose, and at times it was all he could do to stop himself from grabbing Cassie's phone and not just texting Lucy but trying to call her, and perhaps she'd be there, that immutable voice sashaying through the cosmic threshold, so pleased to hear from him, so much to say. He'd smile – the first time in many months – and feel the lightness of joy, the wondrous return of all that was lost, never to be recovered yet found again, the worst of dreams and now the waking from it, to the beauty of normal life. But the line was fragile, Cassie and he recognised this without the other having to warn them. Efficient, controlled ... yes, a chip off the block. They were not to rush Lucy, nor to force her to speak. She, who had been so chatty and vivacious in life – it was their honour to wait on her now. To try to call would be to muddy the waters through which she was managing to communicate, creating a murk that may make it impossible for further contact – a catastrophe. So Hugo sat in his chair with his coffee, staring out across the field behind the house, waiting. And Cassie would continue to read her books, to watch the many videos she'd made of Lucy, and let the flute sit mute.

Soon there was no more talk of the eleven-year-old going to live with her aunt. This may have given the nerves of the father and the daughter a rest, but for Arlene, a sense of life having thwarted her yet again nagged at the edges of all she should be grateful for. She hadn't set out to steal Cassie from Hugo – the thought wouldn't have entered her mind had his cold shoulder not become so brutal, or had Cassie seemed able to cope with being blamed by her father for stealing Lucy. But somewhere along the line she'd started to think of Cassie as, if not her daughter, then her responsibility, which may amount to the same thing. She'd loved how that felt. How pleasant the burden of the child upon shoulders so often called selfish, especially by her ex-husband (that foul alcoholic merchant of pig swill).

Not that she was indiscriminate in her affections, and any kid would do. Cassie was special, not just because she was her niece. She'd coped with a miserable year miraculously well, and was such fun to be with! The more time Arlene spent with her, the more time she wanted to spend. Of course, now she was a central part of Hugo and Cassie's lives – but it wasn't what it could have been – what it almost was. She was unimpressed with the current arrangement. The fact that there'd been no word from "Lucy" since the second text had been disregarded by the "true believers", who appeared to be ready to wait for ever. Neither Hugo nor even Cassie would thank her for the reality check, but maybe ... in a decade's time ... if Arlene did stick her oar in, then they'd realise she'd stopped them from dragging one another to an insanity they'd never return from, or maybe she'd lose them both forever.

And so Arlene sat, in the lawyer's office. `You have to help me,` she said. `Please, will you come?`

`Of course,` Faro replied, saddened, musing. `Strangers who know each other ... That it should come to this. If Lucy only knew...`

`It would break her heart.`

The heaviness of the law office lay its gloom upon the room. Both Arlene and Faro had experienced bad news and bad vibes in these walls, but nothing as awful as the prospect of the woman for whom nothing was more important than her husband and her daughter having left behind an ice cold cocoon; encased within it, those two very people in what Arlene feared may be a death spiral. Chronically depressing, they agreed without speaking the course of action they'd take, in equal parts natural, opaque, humanitarian and full of well-intentioned deceit.

Arlene continued to make a presence of herself in the house of cautious hope. And yet another day passed with zero word from the great beyond. Routines fallen into continued without question; silence was broken by the conversation of the two women, older and younger. Hugo merged with the background. They spoke, about what neither would have been able to recall; the ebb and flow of their chat, a couple of hours at least before it was time to get things ready. On arrival, Arlene had said, `Andrew's coming over. It's been a while since you saw him; I know how much you like him, Cassie ...`

`I do, I do!` the eleven-year-old exclaimed.

`I thought we could use some extra conversation,` she continued, noting Hugo's discomfort at the prospect, despite his outward impassivity. `And he promised he wouldn't charge.` Cassie chuckled heartily, but her father clearly hid an element of concern about this guest. Arlene was wondering what Hugo may have said to Faro, a man he'd been happy to mix with in the past. `It'll be good for you,` she concluded, adding without apparent irony: `While you wait for Lucy.`

The lawyer arrived with bottles of red and white wine and a calm face masking his concern over the state of the family he was so fond of. He was warmly welcomed by Cassie and Arlene. Hugo was already sat at the dining table. `Hello,` Faro said as he came in to the house. From the distance, his putative host gave one of those little nods people muster when trying hard to be civil, but the effort was too great. A veteran of far worse personalities than this, Faro recognised the struggle.

The convivial pre-dinner conversation took place mostly in the kitchen, and focused on everyone but the mute, who didn't move from the table, where he solemnly sat, gradually joined by the others as the feast took to the skies.

`This is delicious!` the lawyer said, tucking into his hefty plate of food.

`I had help,` Arlene replied, smiling at her niece. The eleven-year-old grinned back.

`Cassie,` Faro said. `Have you decided what you want to be when you grow up? Would you'd like to come work for me?`

`I don't know what I want to do ...` she replied. `Before Mum died I was thinking I might like to be an actress. Now ... possibly something medical.`

`I'm sure whatever you do,` he replied, `You'll be an amazing and fantastic success.`

`She's so smart,` Arlene explained, bubbling with pride. `She reads books I was struggling with when I was 25! I took her to see the Picasso exhibition.`

`It was awesome!` Cassie said.

`Little did I know I'd gone with the art critic of The New Yorker - she was all over those pictures!`

`So you're a fan of Cubism?` Faro asked.

Cassie nodded vigorously. `Arlene got me this beautiful book when we finished. I've been studying it non-stop!`

`I know what to get you for your birthday,` the lawyer said.

`Did you go to the show?` Arlene asked Faro.

`Not yet, but I intend to.`

`Tell me!` Cassie said. `I'll come with you!`

`That would be my pleasure,` he replied.

`You'll learn far more from her than from any of those audio guides,` said Arlene, her cup of pride runnething over.

It was as if the silent, brooding Hugo wasn't there, yet a fourth sat at the table. Every now and then, they'd try to include him in the conversation, and he'd try to be included, but despite the effort, it remained a party of three with a shadow of one.

The stand-out superstar of the evening was the little girl, and a little more than a little girl, a little grown up. Increasingly confident, about her subject, and a little more than that. `Arlene bought me this book about a brilliant architect who designed these incredible buildings in Barcelona,` she explained, eleven going on thirty seven. `The biggest is this huuuuge cathedral that looks like a spaceship landed from Planet Cool, and is sitting there ready to eat you all up! It still isn't finished, they've been building it for over a hundred years, can you believe that?!! And there are these other places around the city, far-out apartment blocks, and one has this roof garden with these really strange and amazing sculptures that look like weird animals! And there's this garden, with alligators and two fairy tale houses and it was supposed to be an enchanted town but they didn't finish it, but there's still this village market place and a big open area where a china snake stretches all the way around and you can sit in it and watch the people pass by! This one guy, Gaudi. I'd love to go there, can we some time?`

Arlene smiled. `Of course, darling. Maybe I'll take you for your birthday.`

The young woman beamed with delight.

A well-behaved guest, the lawyer helped Arlene clear up. Hugo and Cassie had been dismissed from the table – Arlene wanted to speak with the visitor in private. `So what do you think?` she asked.

They'd only touched briefly on the matter at hand over dinner, in such a negligible manner those not looking wouldn't have noticed. Faro was not yet supposed to know the whole truth, but he had picked up on the vibes any way. `They really believe it ...` he said. `That Lucy would still be conscious ... Aware ... Watching over them from the 30th floor of a skyscraper ... If it was just Hugo, I'd have said he was mad. But Cassie too? I know how much Lucy loved her, how frightened she was about leaving ...`

`Andrew: we have to do something.`

`What do you think?`

`If she stays in the house much longer ...?`

`It's her home ...`

`What, with Hugo???`

`He's her father.`

`He's a joke!`

`But where would she live?`

`With me.`

It blurted out, sounding as if the whole evening had been predicated upon this chance to make her case. Faro fell silent. At first flush, she seemed ashamed, but despite his bonhomie, and having enjoyed the evening, he'd come for a reason too. `Hugo and Cassie have been under so much pressure lately,` he said. `It's obvious why, and I wouldn't expect anything else. In his own mute way, Hugo was devoted to Lucy, while Cassie and she were inseparable. They have every right to go a bit crazy, and for a while. Arlene, you've been taking the strain. To be honest, I'm most worried about you.`

She stopped loading the dishwasher, and looked at him with a slanted, angry expression.

Faro continued to put condiments away as he spoke. `I was worried about you the day you came to my office, and I've been worried about you tonight.`

`Tonight???`

`You've sparkled, but I could see the strain in your eyes, the concentration. Are you disappointed Hugo is back in his shell?`

`I'm used to it,` she replied, coolly.

`But Cassie is doing well. And a lot of that is down to you.`

Her silence indicated she agreed with that.

`You've done a great job,` he said. `She needed you. Without you around then ...`

`It's been ... no trouble at all.`

`You love her,` Faro said.

She nodded.

`Are you disgruntled that ... after all of this ... she's still not ... unh, how should I put it? Still not with you – full time?`

She looked away.

`But she needs her father,` Faro said, with sympathetic honesty. `And, Lord alone knows, though he'd never find the words, he desperately needs her. He's not mad, Arlene, and he's not going mad. It might take him a long time, her too, but time is what they have. So you know what my advice is?`

`What?` she replied.

`Let them be.`

She turned back towards him, and wiped her eyes. She said nothing, glowering at him. `Andrew,` she said finally, `This is not the kind of counsel I brought you here to provide.`

With a smile, he said, `I know.`

11

Mid-Sunday morning, the sun shining through the window, Cassie lay on her bed, half-reading, half-thinking about her twelfth birthday, just around the corner. She thought of her auntie, whose mood had saddened in recent weeks. She knew why, she knew how, and appreciated the restraint Arlene had exercised upon her own disappointment. If a part of growing up was the inevitability of letting down others, Cassie had stumbled miserably through her first experience of being the one to do the letting down. Yet Arlene had said nothing, had remained the same loving aunt, the same great mate, and now the sadness was lessening, much to her relief. She knew how strong Arlene had been for her throughout this period. She wouldn't forget that for as long as she lived.

An unexpected knock at her bedroom door. There was only one person it could be, and sure enough, when she opened up: Hugo. The same dude, the same face, but this morning he seemed a little different, though she couldn't place how or why.

And then, as she realised, he said: `No texts?`

Cassie shook her head. `I'd have let you know.`

Normally at this point, he'd have walked back to whichever hole he'd come from. But now he lingered. He said: `Do you want some brunch?`

For a moment, she stared at him. And then: `Unh ... Okay.`

They settled in a nearby bruncherie. Sunday morning cool, the locale well-chosen, relaxed and pleasant, the food good and familiar. Cassie recalled past brunches in this eatery years ago, a brief phase of Lucy's, determined by Hugo's schedule. Cassie was smaller then, but the bruncherie remained welcoming and friendly, and the food not so distant from her palate's recollection. Yet despite the fondly flavoured past and apparently chilled current, they'd have looked to outsiders a somewhat odd arrangement. Hugo sat reading several newspapers, appearing to ignore Cassie, while Cassie watched the goings-on around them, appearing to ignore Hugo. Every now and then she looked at her father, who silently made his way through a large fried breakfast, two cups of coffee and orange juice, his face impassive, his expression a blank. Then she'd go back to watching the couples around them, the families and friends indulging in the serious business of a late breakfast. He was oblivious to their surroundings, but she'd notice him look up at someone in the distance for a moment before settling down again, back to the papers. Set amongst this vista of normality, the eleven-year-old had the pleasant sensation that they were in fact normal. She wondered how many more of those who came for brunch were equally keen to maintain a pretence that they were more grounded than they were, probably far less grounded than they needed to be.

Her phone took pole position on the table by her plate. A text came from one of her friends. Cassie responded with rapid-tapping fingers. Waiting for a reply, she watched an amusing stream of footage of she and Lucy on a road trip in the months before her death, one of her favourites. She'd seen it many times: her mother's antics always made her chuckle. Hugo looked up from his paper at his randomly laughing daughter. He stared at her. She cued the footage and handed him the phone. `Watch this,` she said. `It's funny.`

He took the phone from her, unaware of what he was about to see. There, on a small screen held in his hand, was a still image of Lucy, radiant despite radiotherapy, her eternal smile beaming into the lens. His daughter motioned that he should press the button to start the film running. As if he were trying to dismantle an atomic bomb, Hugo set the footage to play, and there, with the sound turned up, was Lucy's voice as she spoke to the eleven-year-old gurgling with delight from behind the phone's camera. His expression didn't change. No glimmer from another star, no emotion at all. When it came to an end, he continued to stare at the screen, Lucy's still image caught in perpetuity until further notice. He handed the phone back to Cassie and returned to his newspaper without comment or note. The eleven-year-old looked at her father for a long long time before shaking her head and continuing her survey of their fellow brunchers.

Later in the afternoon, she was in her room, awake after a post-brunch nap. Her flute in its box, unplayed; her reading close to hand, untouched. She mulled upon Hugo's behaviour. He didn't react to the footage of Lucy, there was no feedback, no triggered reminiscence, not even the occasional light sigh. He'd watched her for a whole minute forty, maybe two minutes; Cassie was certain it was the first time he'd seen his dead wife "alive" since her demise. Sure, maybe he was a little shocked at first, maybe there was some deep inner reflection, but at the end of it – when passing back the phone – there should at least have been something! Some kind of remark, or note, or observation! A trace, an echo of a reaction to the woman who'd been his consort and soul mate for all those years, and with whom he'd planned to spend the rest of his time on Earth, maybe a further five or six decades! But nothing. All that time, staring at her face and there was nothing he wanted to say, directly or by accident, to the child of that union, to the last remain vestige of the woman to whom he'd purportedly devoted everything. He was still a man in an emotional coma. A fascinating specimen if she were a psychiatrist and he of no relation; an infuriating burden in actuality. Her mother said that Cassie needed him, yet he remained without need of anything but Lucy. The contamination burnt her again, each time deeper.

Arlene was coming over for dinner to talk about their trip to Barcelona and perhaps elsewhere in Spain. The prospect of seeing not only Gaudi's buildings but Picasso's paintings was beyond thrilling! After witnessing Hugo's profound non-reaction to her footage of Lucy, her aunt's unspoken understanding that Cassie would not be going to live with her powered a feeling that Cassie absolutely should go and live with her, her future happier, kinder, warmer, more gentle, more affectionate, more fun, more educational, more everything if she resided with her human and humane aunt instead of her lifeless father. Soon to be twelve, Cassie needed to feel she was not a burden by wanting to have a two-way relationship with the key people in her life. She feared growing into a cold dead woman if forced to behave like a cold dead child.

Another unanticipated knock at her door. She called out, `Come in.`

Hugo entered.

Cassie shook her head. `No texts.`

He nodded his acknowledgement, then said, `I was ... hoping ... I mean I didn't come up here just to ask about the texts. I was wondering ... Can I ... watch some of the ... other ... videos you have of your ... mother?`

He'd never asked before, and now she came to think of it, until this morning she'd never offered. Maddeningly formal though he was, Cassie recognised her oversight, and felt morally compelled to correct it. `Dad, I've got loads of film of her.` She slid off her bed and walked to her computer. `Go get something to sit on.`

By the time Hugo returned with a chair, Cassie had loaded up several videos of she and Lucy chatting, shopping, being serious, cracking up. Hugo sat next to her as she played short takes lasting seconds – chaotic, hysterical, moments – and longer: ten, twenty minutes, sometimes specific events shot for specific reasons, others simply to immortalise the air they breathed. Hugo watched in silence. Soon an hour passed, then two, in which the father and the daughter sat together without making a noise, watching Lucy dance and rant and gossip and expound and blather and do voices and mimic Hugo and bake cakes and illustrate unfairnesses and try to play the flute badly and list her ten favourite songs and divulge her hopes for Cassie. One could start watching these videos just for a few moments, a couple of minutes at most, and find oneself drawn into the adventure the footage recorded for much longer than that, as if one were there, as if you could feel the breeze across the hill just climbed, the centuries contained within the stone the old fortress sojourned to; and then the discussion, the asides, the digressions – you'd be nodding in agreement at an amusing comment made at the time, recorded on the video, knowing that had you been there you'd have nodded in the exact same way you were doing now; and the sight of food across a restaurant table, and desserts in particular, grand conurbations of sugar and chocolate sauce, all for the delicate delight in the company of loved ones; and in the good vibes of the bonhomie of a wonderful time cocooned in the capsule of video, you were almost there yourself.

He chuckled.

Cassie looked at him in shock. He didn't feel her gaze; he was still warmed by the embers of a laugh raised by Lucy's impression of him. He hadn't see her do that since their early days together, before she'd been affected by respect for his seriousness, and thought it no longer appropriate. Cassie let the video play through before making a mental note of that particular film and loading up another.

They were still sitting there when it was dark. The distant thud of the front door reminded them that Arlene was coming over for dinner.

Cassie said, `We'd better stop.`

Hugo said. `Can we do this tomorrow?`

`Of course.` With that, she turned off her computer and they went to greet Arlene. Her aunt was as excited about their trip to Barcelona as she was, and had brought numerous books, guides and travel notes. `We can make it a voyage around Catalonia!` she said. `You must read this book by Orwell.` The whole dinner conversation was taken up by their plans. Hugo again sat in silence, never once offering an unsolicited comment or gesture that could be mistaken as such.

In her excitement at their expedition, which increased with each passing sentence, Cassie was seized by a fit of babbling. When the words started flooding out and it was clear what was about to happen, she looked at Arlene with alarm, who looked back at her with equal concern. They both looked at Hugo, whose eyes were turning on his apparently-possessed child with their familiar malignant frostiness, the undertone of menace. The memory of his last explosion was present in their minds, an impact driven hard, a force that shook them all, the house too. It became clear how fragile the eco-system of this mausoleum remained, Hugo's impending explosion the touch fire, the end. Such thoughts ran through Cassie's mind as useless words came burbling out.

`Ireallylikestainedglasswindowsthecoloursaresoop rettyandthepicturesareoftenveryinterestingcontainin gallkindsofstoriesaboutreligionandhistory myfavouritesareinthosemassivecathedralswherethe windowisalmostthesizeof ...`

Frozen as they waited for the outburst, no excuse, bang to rights, I hate this and you know I do. The only movement: from Cassie's unstoppable lips, fluttering away in flowery ignorance of the doom about to fall; she herself turning red with frustration, dread anticipation, a fatal inability to rein in the babbles. Arlene as well, despite her bravado, despite her disdain: secretly terrified of a nuclear Hugo, of the bomb so rarely dropped; the painful ticking down of the last few seconds before the end of all things, before the fracturing into too many fragments for a successful re-assembly ever to take place. Five ... four ... three ... two ...

`Let it out,` Hugo said, calmly. `We'll wait until you're finished.`

A flash of relief passed through the room, a nuclear blast – but good. Following the moment, an instant replay, the fall-out – but good. Cassie and Arlene exchanged glances, recording this massive event, a sudden alteration, a sea change, the world leaping to a happier motion with no notice whatsoever – but the child still had to endure, and so with remarkable composure, the three sat at the dinner table waiting for the soon-to-be-twelve-year-old to expunge all that needed to come out. As ever, an erudite, random selection of subjects, but with the anxiety removed, it wasn't the same burden, nor had the same devastating impact on the little girl. Sitting at the table, waiting for her babbling to end, a commune of the reasonable, and still the immense surprise. Hugo almost like Buddha, contemplating, calm. After fifteen minutes, the verbal splurge was over. Cassie felt wearied but nowhere near as shattered as usual. Arlene asked if she was okay. She replied that she was. And they continued with dinner, as if nothing had happened.

Later, aunt and niece spoke out of Hugo's earshot. `I can't believe it,` Arlene said. `I was waiting for him to go nuts.`

`Me too,` Cassie replied.

`Strange,` aunt concluded.

`Very strange,` niece agreed.

The following morning brought a new routine between father and daughter. The question of any texts from Lucy; the response in the negative; the taking care of necessary chores, including the consumption of food; the adjourning to Cassie's bedroom to watch more of the footage she'd made of Lucy before and after the diagnosis. Hugo had barely seen any of it, but his daughter herself had been unable to watch many of the pieces since her mother had died, so it was a voyage for her too, of reminiscence, of recent events, of great happiness amongst the desperation, the anticipation of loss. Strangely, she found she was able to enjoy this footage more freely than she had when making it, when Lucy was still there. The child lived those last six months knowing exactly what was going to happen to her mother, knowing the brutal tug of the living from the face of the Earth was yet to occur, and when it did, she'd feel as if she too was being yanked from the sentient universe. Having endured this horrendousness the first time around, she could watch the footage knowing that her mother was no longer suffering. She didn't have to feel guilty about her own good health while Lucy was being eaten alive from the inside by a voracious, unstoppable disease housed in her cells. Now she could see what she hadn't noticed: a grimace, a sigh, a momentary glaze in the eyes as pain gripped hold; how her mother was trying so hard to hide the worst of it. She'd have been pleased to be so successful in this venture, though there were many occasions when Cassie noticed her mother's pain but didn't let on. Even so, after watching a few hours of footage, Cassie would be streaming tears at her mother's bravery, yet still Hugo would sit there, stone-faced. After bearing a sterile countenance, he'd stand up, ask Cassie if she'd like to go and get some lunch (or dinner if it had been that long), and she would or she wouldn't, and they'd go and get food or Hugo would leave her alone. And when he was gone, she would think, how can you sit there for all that time as if you were in a business meeting??? There she is! Her image, her sound, her smile, her sense of humour! React, dammit, react!!! But there was no glimmer from him of anything other than a dismal automaton, the only chuckle she'd seen clearly a glitch, a twitch, an involuntary manoeuvre that had no counterpart, no successor. How much longer would she have to sit with him watching hours of footage before there'd be a second chuckle, or – heaven forbid – a laugh?

Cassie was getting ready for bed, furious with Hugo over his vacant, insipid audience response. The last thing she wanted to do was go and say goodnight to him. Yet she felt impelled to by Lucy's text. Perhaps Hugo suffered the same pressure, which is why she so often felt short-changed by his invisible attempts at attention. With the angry weariness of the duty-bound, she found Hugo sitting in his chair, espresso cup in hand, staring out into the darkened field. It took him a few moments to notice she was there. When he looked at her, he asked the inevitable question. `Any texts?`

She shook her head. He nodded, okay. She was ready to dart back to her room to nurture her anger at him, but then paused. As she stared, Cassie realised that her father was actually quite a handsome man. It had never occurred to her before, but she could see why her mother may have fallen in love with him, despite his difficult ways. Unable to stop herself, she blurted: `Tell me about her.`

He looked at Cassie, surprised. But his face was open, rather than shut down. She waited in a state of uncertainty. And then he nodded to the chair nearby. She sat, as quickly as possible, lest he change his mind and dismiss her to sleep.

`What do you want to know?` he asked.

`Tell me how you felt the first time you saw her.`

`The first time I saw Lucy ...` he said. `She was working on a project with someone at my firm. I came in – and there she was, yammering away in an office a few doors along from mine. I walked past and noticed her out of the corner of my eye. I didn't see her full-on, I didn't turn my head, I kept on walking. But my heart started to beat faster than if I'd ran a thousand metre sprint. I sat down at my desk. Instead of getting straight to work, I just sat there, totally still apart from my pulse, thinking that a few paces away from me was the most amazing woman I had ever seen. And I wanted to stand up and go into her office and talk to her, but I couldn't move. My legs had frozen, I felt I'd suffocate if I didn't go and see her, and I'd suffocate if I did. I'd never felt like that in my life about anyone. The famous ... bolt from the blue. A legend. A lie. But there was I, not knowing what to do. Utterly ridiculous – I hadn't even seen her properly. I heard a knock on the frame of my open door. I looked up, and there she was. I saw her properly, and every sensation I'd felt as I passed by her was confirmed ten times over now there was nothing between us, no furniture or walls, no space. She introduced herself, as it looked like I might be involved on her project too. And before she shook my hand I knew I'd just met the only woman I'd ever love.`

Cassie sat, her eyes wide open.

He looked out of the window, at the dark field, at eternity. `Dear God,` he breathed. `I miss her so much.`

12

More days passed, and weeks, and still there was no third text message from Lucy. Father and daughter began to wonder, and for a long time daren't say to the other what each was starting to think. Hugo would ask, `Any texts?` and Cassie would shake her head. They'd say no more than that, until later on or the following morning, and the question once again, and the answer.

`I need a change of scenery,` he said, following yet another negative response. `How about we go out?`

She was surprised and perturbed by the offer. But the surprise outweighed the perturbedness.

She agreed.

They were in the car for an hour. Cassie tried to make conversation, but it flickered and failed under the pressure of her father's domineering silence. Their destination was a forest, a mystical, mysterious locale, vivid in the grasp of the right imagination, but about which Hugo only said, `I came here a few times with your mother, long ago.` Evidently it was up to Cassie to provide the imagination. Together they walked through the woodland, branches creating cool pools of shade before shafts of light returned them to the vibrant world. The taller trees made crazy shadows along the ground, drawing her to distant lands when the silence in this one became too onerous. She'd been moved by her father's exhalation but like a shark, the fin of his feeling had emerged only briefly before vanishing beneath the surface, to emerge next who knew when?

The decline of her hope appeared as a sudden rotting fruit: obvious when viewed in fast motion. With admirable loyalty to her mother's cosmic request, Cassie had tried time and again to fight the notion that her father really was incapable of expressing anything more than the tiniest sliver of emotion. They were bonded in their mutual anticipation, but if there was to be no third text from Lucy, what did that mean for the second text, and the obligation it contained? She could go back and forth over this point, but her father was never going to be anything more than an automaton, and she had to escape him before he made her one too.

For the next few days, she watched Hugo, knowing that sub-consciously she had decided to make the move, and leap after all into Arlene's willing arms and the warm, loving, communicative home she could offer. He had no idea that she was contemplating a departure; why would he? He hadn't even noticed how she'd grown these last few months, though she was ever-present before him.

The phone rang. Hugo answered it. `Hello?`

`Ah! I'm glad it's you, I was hoping it would be.`

`Andrew.`

`Do you have a moment? It's ... a delicate matter. Because I know you think I'm a non-believer. I'd love to ... but ...`

`What is it?`

`It's something Cassie asked me about a while ago. I didn't think much of it then, although it was a strange query ... And when I had dinner at your's recently, and she was talking about ... the texts.`

`Yes?`

`Well ... I thought I should look into it more deeply. So I called the phone company that provided the number Lucy used to have. I asked him about the texts Cassie received.`

`You did?`

`Yeah,` Faro replied, noting with dismay the excitement creeping into his old friend's voice. He had to get this out quickly. `They said that sometimes you can send a text and it gets caught up in the system, it stays there until suddenly it gets dislodged, at which point it's finally delivered. The delay can be seconds ... minutes ... hours ... days ...` Faro's voice trailed off, an apologetic wisp at its edge.

After a glum pause, Hugo finished off the sentence: `Weeks ... months ...`

`Yeah ...` Faro said, beaten and disloyal.

There was a long silence before Hugo said, `You think ... Lucy sent ... Cassie those ... texts ... before ... she died?`

`No one would be happier than me if it turned out I was wrong but ...`

`Well, Andrew ... I think ... Cassie and I would probably ... be happier than you.`

`Yeah ... I'm sure ... you would be.`

Another long silence. A doleful zilch emanating from Hugo's end of the line. The bereaved man's internal monologue: a stillness within a hush within an iceberg within a scream. Oppressive. Dissolving the lawyer's ear, pressed against the phone.

`I'm sorry,` Faro said, the bearer of bad news, he knew – but bad news with a purpose. The lawyer told himself, Arlene's the one who'll understand. `Listen, I've got to go. But I'm here, okay? Call me any time, we can speak if ... unh ... that's what you want to do. But if not ... well, I'm here any way.`

Hugo put the phone down, numb. Stood still. Thought. Thought some more. It didn't make sense. But it did. A sound of ... what in Faro's voice: vindication? A deft lawyer's trick: compromise Cassie's contact with Lucy and therefore torpedo the veracity of the message contained within the lipstick book? Those texts had to be real. It all had to be real. For if one part was not, then ...

Hugo suddenly became aware; he looked up. Cassie was watching him. On her face, a grasp of the content of the conversation he'd just had with Faro.

She said, `There's not going to be any more texts, is there.`

He didn't know what to do. He couldn't bring himself to think that; he certainly couldn't expect Cassie to as well. But, putting aside the theories of how such personal texts came to find her phone, it was utterly convincing. He found himself shaking his head, though he could hardly believe it himself.

She said, 'She's not coming back, is she?'

An epochal pause. He stared at her.

She had cried often, sobbed her little heart out, broke her little self into little bits on many previous occasions. But now, when the truth that will out had out, a couple of days before her twelfth birthday, the news accrued to its logical conclusion, and she felt calm. She realised that she'd grieved already, had let out all that had to come out at this stage. The final one percent of the realisation that her mother was gone forever proved to be a step she could cover without taking a pace. Sure, she'd cry again in the future, as one did for the ever-lost, but the first phase was over, she knew this now.

Hugo wavered, tried to find his chair, missed it and dropped to the floor, a dead weight.

'Dad!' she yelped.

He'd fainted, and woke moments later with tears pouring from his eyes, babbling with a hysteria she could barely decipher. 'Lucy, Lucy, I'm so sorry, I let you down so badly. I thought we'd have so much LONGER than we did, I was trying so hard, I wanted to be everything TO you but I fell so short, and NOW I'VE lost you, AND there's nothing more, NOTHING LEFT, ALL I WANTED TO BE, ALL I WANTED TO SAY, this is … I WISH WE HAD MORE TIME, I could have been a more giving person, more open, I'M SO SORRY LUCY, PLEASE FORGIVE ME, I CAN'T SURVIVE WITHOUT YOU, I CAN'T SURVIVE WITHOUT KNOWING YOU DIDN'T HATE ME, THAT I WASN'T SUCH A TERRIBLE DISAPPOINTMENT. PLEASE, I'm so sorry, I need you so much, I miss you SO MUCH, I didn't know we'd RUN OUT OF TIME, I tried MY best, I tried to be A GOOD husband and father, Lucy, I'm so sorry, I'm so sorry, please forgive me, LUCY, please forgive me, please forgive me.`

Exhausted, his eyes rolled back in their sockets. He fainted again. Still on the floor where Cassie was cradling him, holding on to him, calming him, soothing him, promising him they were past the worst of it. She knew she wouldn't be able to lift him, so she carefully lowered him from her lap to the floor, and went running to get a pillow and duvet. When she came back, she put the pillow beneath his head, gently resting him back down; covered him up to his neck, put on the T.V. and sat in a chair nearby to keep a close eye on him.

The admonition from her mother: your father needs you. A text it seemed that Lucy had sent just before she died. A text that came from someone no longer here, neither in the great beyond nor nearby, nor looking over her shoulder to make sure she didn't put a foot wrong. An admonition typed in the last few hours of her life, each letter agonised but essential, sent to her daughter, one of the last things on her mind before she met with her end, the end that really was the end, and not just the end of this life before the beginning of the next, but the end of all life, all existence, all consciousness, now and forever, until the end of the end of time. Her last chance to say what was on her mind.

As he slept, exhausted all the way down to his core, Cassie could see now that Lucy had been right to appoint her Hugo's guardian, to send those last texts – one to her, one for her to take note of – that were destined to be held by an ironic, cruel universe for months, landing with their recipient long after they were supposed to. How creative could be the misery inflicted on the innocent! How little there could be to appeal against.

Time passed. Hugo woke, surprised not only to find himself on the floor of the lounge but also covered in a duvet with a pillow beneath his head. His surprise was enlarged by how comfortable he was. He laid his head back down for a while, enjoying the restful nature of his crib. But he needed coffee. Slowly he sat up, and only now did he see Cassie asleep on the chair nearby. It was dark outside; it might have been the middle of the night, or just before dawn. She looked uncomfortable. He stood, and bundled up the duvet so that he may lay it over her, so she too would be cosy. He could try to take her up to bed, but didn't know what time she'd dropped off, how deep in a sleep she may be. He didn't want to disturb her – better she should rest.

At that moment, she began to stir. Cassie saw him in the process of picking up the duvet, bringing it over to her. When he saw she'd woken, he put the duvet down and walked to the chair on which she sat. He held open his arms. She was still for a moment – and then leapt into the first fatherly hug she could recall for many a miserable time. She threw her arms around him. He embraced her. And they stood as the sun came up.

In the morning, they sat together in the kitchen, having silently prepared breakfast. While they ate, they agreed how nice it would be to invite Arlene out for the day. Her auntie was thrilled by the offer.

`Where are we going?` Arlene asked, the voice transmitted by the phone heartened to such an extent that Cassie realised she had made her day.

`For a walk,` she replied. `And then lunch.`

But then came a pause. Cassie felt the hairs on the back of her neck rise. Arlene said, `You're sure?`

`Of course!`

`I mean ... I'm not going to get in the way?`

`You're my good angel,` Cassie said. `How could you ever get in the way?`

Arlene's voice choked. `Darling: thank you.`

The eleven-year-old relayed her aunt's acceptance to her father, who nodded. As they finished breakfast, she noticed that some of the lines had fallen from his face, and the line of his jaw seemed a little less set. He was handsomer, and chatty this morning, at least by his own standards, talking about the videos they'd watched of Lucy, about snippets he could recall of Barcelona, told to him by people he knew who'd been there. Even the house seemed to have sighed relief; Hugo's outpouring had doused the walls with vulnerability, a watering of dried and dusty land that was tending towards tundra. The light shining on this morning no longer seemed to crack the parched planes of the estate.

They ambled peacefully over to Arlene's abode, her father's better mood still present and vital. The trio wandered on through the forest, across which there lay a funky pub, servant of food and bonhomie. On the way, beneath the canopies of trees, they spoke of the village Arlene had taken Cassie to, of Hugo's memories of being there when they were younger – some of which failed to tally with her aunt's recollection of events. Cassie noted this discrepancy with forensic amusement, but decided not to comment, despite a few amused glances exchanged with Arlene.

Lunch was plush. Quick and perceptive, Arlene could see the change in both father and daughter, and though she didn't know what had happened, she was aware of a massive improvement. Which clearly deserved celebration. `Why don't we have wine?` she said. `After all, it's Cassie's birthday tomorrow, and she won't have time to celebrate seeing as she'll be packing so she can come with me to Barcelona.`

Hugo nodded, and there was a trace of a smile – in fact there was more than a trace of a smile, there was an actual smile. Cassie squealed with excitement. He called over the waiter, ordered three glasses of wine. `And three for me too!` the almost-twelve-year-old said, her auntie laughing loudly, her father still – miraculously – smiling.

Out in the sunshine, after lunch, the town was relaxed and bijou. Cassie and Arlene walked slightly ahead of Hugo, deep in the conversation of conspirators. His favourite second hand book shop was about to arrive.

`Hey,` he called out.

The two women stopped and looked back at him.

`I'm just going in here,` he said, nodding at the book shop.

Arlene replied, `We're heading to Medina's,` a shoe shop further along the road. `Whoever's finished first, come and join the others.`

He nodded. The lunch party temporarily divided along gender lines to cater for special interests.

In the book shop, the familiar aroma of nurturing tomes welcomed him into cool, hidden corners surrounded by learned shelves. He knew the stock well, could tell the latest arrivals amongst the volumes. A couple of books he'd been thinking about getting the last time he was here – he was heading to the first one when a new arrival caught his eye.

He stopped dead. A book he recognised. A book he'd read. A book he'd once owned.

A book he'd given away. In Australia.

He began to shake as he reached out, lifted the book from the shelf. The trembling grew as he took it in both hands. A book years old, though still in reasonable shape. He opened it up, turned the pages.

To page 17 ... to page 41 ...

Familiar story, themes, the texture of the paper, the font of the words ...

To page 67 ... to page 79 ...

And now he could barely control his hands they were shaking so much – he had to be careful not to rip the paper.

To page 91.

To page 93.

To page 95.

Hugo was a mess as he turned the next page, a mess that trebled when he saw a large fulsome lipstick print reaching across page 96. The familiar shape of the lips, the slightly faded texture that spoke of years gone by.

The lipstick sliced through a paragraph that said: 'And so, you go – go and don't come back – for I will never forgive the music you played that night, how good it sounded, and the lights and slights, I will never forgive the crimes you told me hadn't been committed, you of all people.`

He read the words plucked out by the lipstick.

You.

Go.

I.

Forgive.

You.

His eyebrows crumpled, his excitement lost some heat. The decoded message: You go I forgive you.

What on earth ...

And then he realised: conflate the first two words.

You. Go.

Yougo.

HUGO!

And so the message read:

Hugo, I forgive you.

There in the book shop, hidden amongst the shelves, water filled his eyes. He gripped the book, staring at her lipstick, staring at her message. A response to his greatest fear, expressed in open for the first time last night, he knew now for sure that, regardless of texts, regardless of a lawyer's disdain: she was nearby, she was watching over them. She had kept her promise made all those years ago.

Printed in Great Britain
by Amazon